BARBARA COMYNS

was born at Bidford-on-Avon, Warwickshire, in 1909. She was mainly educated by governesses until she went to art schools in Stratford-on-Avon and London. She has worked in an advertising agency, a typewriting bureau, dealt in old cars and antique furniture, bred poodles, converted and let flats and has exhibited pictures in The London Group. She was married first in 1931, to an artist, and for the second time in 1945. She and her second husband lived in Spain for eighteen years.

She started writing fiction at the age of ten and her first novel, *Sisters by a River*, was published in 1947. Since then she has published seven novels: *Our Spoons Came From Woolworths* (1950), *Who was Changed and Who was Dead* (1955), *The Vet's Daughter* (1959), *The Skin Chairs* (1962), *Birds in Tiny Cages* (1964), *A Touch of Mistletoe* (1967) and *The Juniper Tree* (1985). She is also the author of *Out of the Red into the Blue* (1960) which describes her time in Spain. *The Vet's Daughter* is her best-known novel, and has been both serialized and dramatised by BBC Radio; it was also turned into a musical called *The Clapham Wonder* by Sandy Wilson of 'The Boy Friend' fame. Barbara Comyns has one son, one daughter and five grandchildren. She lives in Twickenham, Middlesex.

Virago publishes *Our Spoons Came From Woolworths*, *The Vet's Daughter*, *Sisters by a River* and *The Skin Chairs* and will publish *Who was Changed and Who was Dead* in 1987.

The
Skin Chairs

BARBARA COMYNS

WITH A NEW INTRODUCTION BY
URSULA HOLDEN

PENGUIN BOOKS – VIRAGO PRESS

Penguin Books
Viking Penguin Inc., 40 West 23rd Street,
New York, New York 10010, U.S.A.
Penguin Books Ltd, Harmondsworth,
Middlesex, England
Penguin Books Australia Ltd, Ringwood,
Victoria, Australia
Penguin Books Canada Limited, 2801 John Street,
Markham, Ontario, Canada L3R 1B4
Penguin Books (N.Z.) Ltd, 182-190 Wairau Road,
Auckland 10, New Zealand

First published in Great Britain by William Heinemann Ltd. 1962

This edition first published in Great Britain by Virago Press Limited 1986

Published in Penguin Books 1987

Printed in Great Britain
by Cox & Wyman of Reading, Berkshire
set in Perpetua

Introduction

The Skin Chairs is Barbara Comyns' sixth novel, written in her early fifties, by which time she had a reputation as a highly original writer. Her off-beat talent and innocent eye earned accolades from Graham Greene. This almost ferocious innocence is evidenced once again in the story of Frances, a ten-year-old child living in the twenties with her mother, two brothers and three sisters.

As in *Sisters by a River* it is written in the first person. The action takes place after the death of the father and the resultant change in the family's fortunes. It is while Frances is staying with her Aunt Lawrence and her cousins Ruby and Grace that she has her first glimpse of the skin chairs, owned by a neighbouring general. Blackish and cracked in places, it is the General's wife who admits to Frances that the chairs are covered in human skin. 'He brought them back with him after the Boer War. Five of them are black man's skins and one white. I believe if you look carefully you can see the difference.'

Frances is repelled and fascinated. Did their souls ever come to see what had happened to their skins or had they forgotten them? Did the workmen who covered the chairs know what gruesome work they were doing? It was 'weirdly mysterious'.

Insecurity resulting from her father's death shows in her dreams.

One night I dreamt that Mother's head had been severed and made into a pork pie. Although it was a pork pie, I could still see it was a dead head. There was another fearful dream that Father was floating down the canal, all enlarged with water, and that eels were living in him.

Drowning and putrescence figure elsewhere in Barbara Comyns' work. In *Sisters by a River* the village people frequently drown. In *Who was Changed and Who was Dead*, the river floods the house, creating devastation.

To prevent her nightmares Frances lies awake, trying to recall every detail of her old home: the yellow rug in the drawing room, pieces of which they used for dolls' wigs; the faded morning-room curtains with monkeys climbing up them; the brass bedstead in the spare room, draped in chintz with its feather mattress which their father used to thump to make a hollow for them to lie in. The smaller the detail the happier Frances feels. She recalls a guinea pig dying in the kitchen and one of the maids holding a mirror to its mouth to see if the breath left a mark. She visualizes the mark. She thinks of home with such concentration that it feels as if her spirit has left her body. It would be hard to improve on such a picture of homesickness.

At the instigation of Aunt Lawrence the family move to a smaller house and comparative penury. The cosy between-the-wars life of servants and governesses which Barbara Comyns excels in describing is over. The sensitive Frances settles to the new life with good humour. Under the supervision of Polly, the practical elder sister, the chores are divided, though the mother is weak and does not adapt easily to their diminished circumstances. She dabs at the few remaining pieces of good furniture with a duster and refuses to be seen carrying a shopping basket. Such a bygone flavour of family life is faintly reminiscent of E. Nesbitt, but *The Skin Chairs* is firmly a book for adults, with deep and occasionally horrifying undertones.

The family endure Sunday lunches at the Lawrence's nearby house, which they dislike, but Frances is irrepressible.

> One of her little kid gloves lay on the sofa beside me and I couldn't resist putting my rather stumpy little hand into it. It looked a lovely little hand in the elegant grey glove. I held it up in admiration and, forgetting where I was, cried: 'Oh! when I'm grown up I'll always wear gloves like this. I'll be a beautiful young widow of eighteen and live in Paris and I'll lift up my beautifully gloved, slender hand and say . . .' But I couldn't think what I'd say. 'I'll say: "Tickets, please."'

Frances, like any child, is alert to smells and colours. When Aunt Lawrence kisses them her soft lips smell of sherry. She then collects her husband and her walking stick before walking away into the rat-coloured December dusk.

Her description of following the extraordinary Mrs Alexander on a quest for some bloodhounds is almost surreal.

> I followed behind, sniffing a most unpleasant smell. If that was what bloodhounds smelt of, I didn't want to have anything to do with them . . . There was a huge mound of rubbish heaped up in a field at the side of the house – rotting vegetables, broken china, thousands of empty tins . . . horns . . . some hoofs and a mountain of slimy ash and hen's manure . . . Some of the broken china looked interesting, particularly the remains of a pink mug with 'Remember me' painted on it and there was a three-legged iron cooking-pot like cannibals use . . . Eventually Mrs Alexander emerged from the back of the house with her wet turban slightly awry and her golden slippers golden no longer, but she was chattering away about buying the farm and breeding bears and other rare animals for zoos and perhaps using it as a music centre as well.

Frances' defencelessness is suggested rather than stated. She is fascinated by mud walls. For reassurance she imagines finding enough mud to build a more permanent house than the ones adults take away. She makes a secret house up a ladder in a mud-walled barn, but it is discovered and spoiled. Barbara, the child in *Sisters by a River*, also has a hide-out, where grown-ups cannot follow, but Frances is a more robust and resolute child. They both share a predilection for the curious. When Mr Blackwell becomes a friend of the family and they visit his home Frances notices a lump coming from her sister Esmé's back.

> For a moment I thought she was becoming deformed, then I saw a piece of white showing below her red pullover. I tentatively gave it a little pull and a lot more white appeared... Mother exclaimed sharply: 'You should have left your nightgown at home!'... Esmé was quite unperturbed and said it must have got caught up in her pullover when she was dressing.

Frances is drawn back to the skin chairs despite her fear of them. It is Friday 13th when she takes Esmé to see them on a dark overcast day. They wonder what it would be like if it rained black rain and both are fearful as they enter the General's house and see the partly opened door through which comes loud breathing.

> There was something very red and white inside – most likely a hassock, I thought, or even a huge cherry pie. Then we saw it was the General's head, and one eye was open and the other shut.

The children hurry away, telling no one. After the General's death Frances feels guilty and responsible and her nightmares return. Where earlier she had made wreaths of hay entwined with flowers for the graves of baby chickens she now visits the General's grave with roses of whitish-green. Barbara Comyns is at her most lyrical in this revelation of Frances' sweet nature. She rescues a hedgehog, worrying about it losing its way or getting squashed. A dog passes with a half-grown rabbit in its mouth. She finds the General's grave and her mind wanders as she tries to tell him that she is sorry. She sees a swallow's nest under the church roof and a robin watching her from a yew tree. 'How bright its rusty breast was against the dark green!' A striped cat with a hunting expression on its face stalks a damp Red Admiral drying its wings on a family tomb. She claps her hands to stop the cat pouncing and as she leaves the churchyard it comes and rubs against her black-stockinged legs. She goes home feeling happier.

Barbara Comyns offsets horror and humour with rhapsodic interludes. When Polly returns home from school, the family assemble on the platform to meet her.

> I saw a bent old woman being helped along the platform by her two daughters. So slow she was and bent forward so that her chin almost touched her stomach, and as she tottered past people looked at her with different expressions on their faces . . . She could not control the spit that was dribbling from her mouth, and every now and then one of the daughters would wipe her lips with a man's handkerchief, staring ahead with the self-conscious, pained faces like the parents of idiot children wear. As I watched the old woman, I realized for the first time that one day I would turn into an old woman and crumble away like a dead leaf.

Frances shows touching concern for the weak and young. Her little sister Clare is born with one hand; Frances wants her to inherit more than the rest of them, because of her handicap. When she meets Jane, the baby of the lovely and neglectful Vanda, Frances' maternal nature blossoms.

> The sister took me upstairs and into a long ward containing clean children of all ages, and there was Jane behind a cretonne screen . . . Seeing her there giving me such a welcome made me realize how fond of her I was. With her thin little face and bright eyes she looked so like a bird, the sort that fall out of their nests far too young.

Unlike the children in *Sisters by a River*, who give vent to aggression towards anyone vulnerable, Frances is never cruel. She even feels sympathy for the wax models in the shop window when they are put into maids' uniforms and their faces look embarrassed. She is relieved when they are changed into winter coats, 'Warm but Smart'.

The dreadful Mrs Alexander tries to monopolize Frances to replace her own dead child. It is, appropriately, the woman's treatment of her pet monkey that drives Frances away.

Then she gently opened the lid of the box. Nothing happened for a moment except a strong smell of monkey . . . Then he leapt at Mrs Alexander with teeth bared, making frightful noises. The next thing I knew she was shouting in the most blood-curdling language . . . She implored me to pull him off, but I was far too frightened and made for the front door. By the time I had reached it she had mastered Beppo and was beating him with the poker, her arms and hands bloody and her turban slipping from her cropped head.

Each of the characters in *The Skin Chairs* matures. The mother stands up to Aunt Lawrence, rendering her ineffectual. Ruby, the cousin, escapes to her own brand of happiness. Frances' sense and good humour prevail and the frail 'mud walls' of childhood are strengthened. Her final and startlingly original scene with the skin chairs makes a fitting ending. The souls of the chairs are pacified and Frances' earlier fears are exorcized.

Barbara Comyns comes from a large family and they lived in the country. Later she worked at a variety of jobs, including selling grand pianos, breeding dogs, posing for artists and becoming a successful artist herself. She exhibited pictures in The London Group. Significantly, in her description of Mrs Alexander's house she mentions a painting by Mark Gertler, an artist who lent undertones of horror to mundane and well-loved subjects.

Sisters by a River is largely autobiographical. Of *The Skin Chairs* Barbara Comyns says, 'Only the skin chairs are true. I saw them.' They can be taken as a symbol of human suffering and the predicaments to which humankind is prone. As Frances says, they are indeed 'weirdly mysterious'.

Ursula Holden, London, 1985

One

A FEW WEEKS after my tenth birthday I was sent to stay with some very horsy relations in Leicestershire. My mother, who had a large family of six children – two boys and four girls – sometimes became tired of us and would dispatch us to any relation who would agree to have one or two of the family to stay. At this time there were only three of us at home, the elder ones being at boarding school; but I think there was some governess trouble and our absence gave Mother a good chance to dismiss the offending governess, whose crime had been over-brightness and teaching us to sound the 'h' in white. It was not a very difficult task to dispose of three children at short notice. The two youngest were sent to Uncle Frederick, Father's brother, who lived in Torquay. They did not like Uncle Frederick or his wife, but at least they would be fortunate enough to see the sea. Living right in the centre of England, we did not often visit it. It was green where we lived and like living in the heart of a lettuce. These horsy relations I was sent to were the Lawrences, my mother's uncle and his wife. I suppose Aunt Lawrence would be considered a good-looking woman, but to me she resembled nothing so much as a grey Persian cat, a spiteful one with a well-cushioned face and cunning but wide-open eyes. There were two girl cousins and a long, lanky boy called Charles. Charles must have been about eighteen at this time, because I remember he had just left his public school and was preparing to devote his life to horses. The girls were called Ruby and Grace. Ruby was about a year older than her brother. Poor thing, she was a nervous and anæmic girl with a lined brow, always plucking at her lip with her frail, blue-veined hand. Ruby was about the most inappropriate name she could have been given – she was named after a favourite chestnut mare. Grace was like her mother and, as she was only three years older than I, I had to share her schoolroom, but fortunately not her lessons. Although I did not trust Grace, she had a sort of fascination for me, partly due to the fact that a few years previously she had had the last joint of one of her fingers pinched off in a door. The severed part of her finger had been found in the waste-paper basket, and her nurse, with great presence of mind, had put it back where it had belonged, and with a little attention from a doctor it had grown again, leaving only the slightest scar.

Tower Hill, my great-uncle's farm, was about twenty miles from our village. It was a bleak place and the air seemed to me to smell of damp clay and soot. Aunt Lawrence had most of the trees in the garden cut down except for a few round the tennis-court, and the garden paths had been covered in dark grey bricks and the flower-beds had high box hedging round them, so that it was almost impossible to see the flowers. The house itself was a square Georgian red-brick affair with a lawn in front of it and iron railings. Perhaps it was quite beautiful in a way, but to me, as a child, it was most unattractive. The main farmyard was all stables with a lawn in the centre where manure should have been. There was little farmyard life, no hens pecking at odd bits of corn: they were all imprisoned behind neat wire in the orchard.

6

There were a few pigs, but no one leant over the sty wall to give them a friendly poke now and again with a stick. The cow-sheds were at the other end of the paddock, attached to the house where the bailiff lived and his wife ran the dairy; it was more like the farms at home there, with stacks of straw, but I wasn't allowed to slide down them.

The horses were really beautiful and I liked to watch the grooms making them glow as if they were made of metal. The grooms seldom talked, because they were always making hissing noises as they worked. The most they would ever say was: 'I remember your mother when she was a little girl about your size.' The grooms all looked the same to me: they were thin, wiry men with pink-brown cheeks and mouse-coloured hair. They could have been any age from thirty-five to sixty-five.

The only meal Grace and I had with the rest of the family was luncheon, otherwise we ate in the schoolroom. In a way this was a relief, but all the same I felt slighted – at home I ate all my meals with the grown-ups unless there was a dinner party. In the schoolroom any hot course was served on those metal-and-china plates with hot water underneath. It was really a sensible way of keeping children's food warm, but I hated those plates and felt it was childish to eat off such things. During the first part of my visit the German governess was away having an operation of some sort and Old Nanny was looking after us, the same nanny who had replaced the tip of Grace's finger. She appeared extremely old to me, as if she would break at any minute, sort of dry and crumbly; even her hands seemed as if covered in chalk, which I thought was caused by her bones crumbling through the skin. She was completely dressed in white and I was terrified of her.

Luncheon downstairs was an ordeal. Aunt Lawrence would sit at the end of the table, wearing grey or blue tweeds and usually with a felt hat on her head. She had a silver toast-rack beside her and would nibble toast from time to time. No one else was allowed to eat toast, even at breakfast, because she couldn't bear the sound of other people's crunching. She often had a half-smile on her face, even when she was annoyed, and she used to shout horsy remarks down the long table to her husband. They seldom saw each other except at meal-times and when they were riding together, which wasn't often. Uncle Lawrence, when he was not riding or in the stable-yard, almost lived in his study. Sometimes I was sent to call him, and I found him stretched out in a deep armchair, completely surrounded by paintings and engravings of horses. Everything in the room appeared to be brown, except a gleaming beaten-copper box with SLIPPERS engraved on it. Uncle Lawrence was rather handsome in a slightly foxy, red-haired way and he had the bluest eyes I have ever seen. He was considered to be witty, and had a charming, drawling voice, but did not speak much except when there were guests. He told one story about a man they all knew who visited their local doctor to have his chest examined, and to the doctor's amazement was wearing women's combinations with compartments for the breasts to go into. Although I did not know any of the people concerned, this story seemed wonderfully funny to me and caused me to have one of those snorting, choking fits, and soup came out of my nose. I would have been banished from the dining-room if it had not been for my cousin Charles coming to my rescue. He was a kind, warm-hearted young man and I always tried to sit next to him if possible. Aunt Lawrence looked when I helped myself to cream, so I only dared to take a little; but Charles would take the silver jug and pour mountains of it all over my apple-tart. When there were visitors Uncle Lawrence would ask: 'Which will you have, Frances, a little pheasant or the hash?' It did not make

8

any difference what I answered, because it was always the hash that came my way.

The first few days at Tower Hill were not too unpleasant. Aunt Lawrence was quite glad to have me there to amuse Grace in her governess's absence. She spent an hour or two every day riding with her mother or one of the grooms, but as it was May there was no hunting. Grace was a restless girl. If we started to walk in one direction, it was soon changed to another, so we never got very far. She was always thinking of excuses to walk up and down the village street to see what was happening. If a man lifted his hat to her as he rode past, she would exclaim: 'Oh, I hate that man! Don't you think he is hideous?' And if I answered that I thought him rather handsome, she would giggle and say: 'How could you?' Then at luncheon she would say to her mother: 'Do you know, Frances has fallen in love with Tommy Nichols [or whatever the young man's name was]. Isn't she awful? And to think she is only ten.' Then she would hold her napkin to her mouth and look over it with arch blue eyes. I became more and more careful of my tongue and only made a bad bloomer one other time that I can remember.

We had been lying on straw, reading in the barn. It was pouring with rain and it was very cosy there in the half-light with the rain beating on the corrugated-iron roof. Grace quickly tired of reading and was soon chattering away about the school she was being sent to in a year or so. When she was sixteen she was going to school in Switzerland. I said that I supposed I would eventually go to the same school my two eldest sisters were already boarding at and added that our father was finding it expensive educating so many children, and there was no chance of us being sent to Switzerland. Grace took the straw she was nibbling from her mouth and remarked: 'I don't think it matters much where you go to school. Mummy says none of you will make

9

good marriages.' Fortunately I held my tongue, although I had to bite it. I had almost said: 'I think we are pretty enough to make good marriages, even if we don't have a wonderful education.' I returned to *The Blue Story Book*, but the words meant nothing to me, I felt so angry. Grace did not seem to notice and went on about marriage. She said how awful it would be if one became an old maid, but on the other hand she did not want children. Then she asked what I would do if I never married. I mumbled that I'd adopt some children and have a dog and live by the sea if possible. Then, becoming more interested, I added that if my sister Esmé had not married either we would live together and have check floors we could play chess and draughts on. She said: 'I can see you have got it all planned, but I don't think you will be able to have all those things because your father won't be able to leave you much money. Daddy will leave me plenty; all the same, I don't want to be an old maid. In fact I'd rather marry a groom, wouldn't you?' I grunted a sort of agreement, although the last man I wanted to marry was a groom, always hissing instead of speaking. Grace startled me by exclaiming: 'Good heavens! I don't know what Mummy will say when she hears you want to marry a groom.' I slammed my book to and protested that it was she who had said she would marry a groom; but I knew it was useless, and during the rest of my stay at Tower Hill I was constantly teased about my preference for grooms, although I kept away from them as much as possible.

When Grace was out riding, it gave me a chance to take the dogs for walks and, although I was not supposed to go farther than the paddock alone, I always did. There was a black house-dog called Floss. She pranced and yapped and I did not like her very much, but there were two dear old spaniels who lived in the yard, and, although they would not take walks by themselves, they liked to accompany me.

I could see why they lived in the yard: it was because their ears smelt really awful, but you did not notice it in the fresh air. Around the farm the landscape was flat and full, but about two miles away there was a canal that the dogs liked to swim in, and there were fields of cowslips, and when I smelt them I remembered they would be making cowslip wine at home. We children did not enjoy the taste of wine much, but it was wonderful to think of all the golden cowslips that had gone into it, like bottled early summer days. I never discovered any bluebell woods on my walks and the lanes lacked the wide, grassy verges sparkling with long-stalked buttercups and cow-parsley that we had in Warwickshire. The ponds, and they were scarce, were full and did not seem to have any pond life – newts, tadpoles or those strange worm creatures that live in muddy banks and all disappear if you hold your hand over them. I have no idea what they are called, but we thought they were enchanting. There was one thing that interested me on my walks, and that was mud walls. Sometimes I would come on an old mud barn. Perhaps the doors had rotted away, but the reddish-brown walls still stood. Then I noticed a few of the cottages were made of mud too and crumbling mud walls enclosed some of the orchards and gardens belonging to large houses. These mud walls had a fascination for me, partly because one of the grooms (when he wasn't hissing) had told me that they were very ancient, and also they gave me the feeling that if only I could find enough mud I could build a house myself. We were always building houses in the wood-pile, but a mud house would be more permanent; no one would want to saw it up.

Occasionally, after tea, Charles would take me shooting with him. We didn't say much as we walked over the fields, but he taught me to distinguish the different voices of birds, not only their songs, but their cries and the comforting twitters they made at the end of the day. He also taught me not to be afraid of bats and how to snap my fingers. I forgot this accomplishment very quickly, though. At the end of my second week at Tower Hill Charles was sent to Brussels for six months to improve his French and I felt very defence-less when he had gone. It was about then that the mattress jokes started.

My father was a lawyer, but instead of practising and perhaps having black deed-boxes containing the private papers of the best country families in his office, he pre-ferred to act as legal adviser to a mattress-making firm in Birmingham. He travelled there by train about five days a week, the gardener driving him to the station in the pony trap, our only mode of conveyance except for some rusty bicycles. We considered it a great treat to be allowed to meet the train when he returned in the evening. Except for Mother, we were all quite happy about Father's connection with mattresses, although none of us had ever seen the factory or the mattresses it produced; but by the Lawrence family, at least the women Lawrences, it was considered a despicable occupation.

A ghastly thing happened every evening. Grace and I had to descend to the drawing-room and kiss the grown-ups good night before we went to bed. Often only Aunt Lawrence and Ruby would be there and we got off lightly, but at other times there were strangers who had to be kissed as well. Sometimes the visitors complimented me or said nice things about me to Aunt Lawrence, who was not at all pleased. Then she would start making jokes about the mattresses. 'Well, run along, darling,' she would purr. 'I hope you sleep well on our uncomfortable beds. We can't all have fathers who make mattresses.' Once, almost in tears, I shouted: 'Well, he doesn't make ours. They are gloriously uncom-fortable,' and everyone laughed. There was a joke about getting Father to advise them about their bedding – 'Do you think he would, darling?' – and another about us all wearing overalls made of black and white mattress ticking – 'Just think of it, these six children all running about like little zebras.' Although Grace sometimes teased me about the mattresses, she was as bored with them as I was; but Ruby, who was bullied and nagged by her mother, was delighted to see anyone else suffering and would wriggle about in her chair, her thin lips, like hungry worms, almost disappearing in a pitiful grin.

Somehow it reached my aunt's ears that I could draw quite well – perhaps the nurse had mentioned it – because one evening she suddenly came out with: 'This child thinks she can draw,' and some of the guests boredly murmured: 'Really', or 'What do you draw, dear?' Dreadfully embarrassed, I muttered: 'I don't think I can draw. I only draw when there isn't anything to do.' But Aunt Lawrence said, 'Nonsense, we all want to see what you can do. Come along now,' and from nowhere she produced a writing-pad and pencil which she must have had in readiness. 'Here you are. Now, what about drawing a knight in armour?' Utterly miserable, I explained that I didn't know how armour went, not well enough to draw. Then Ruby chimed in with: 'What about drawing Aunt Flo?' Even in front of all these people I didn't mind drawing Aunt Flo. I was good at caricature and she was easy. I drew her hair parted down the centre and piled into a bun at the back of her head, the slightly protruding teeth, the velvet band round her neck and the strange growth she had on one cheek, the sort of thing that grows on cacti. I handed the finished drawing to Ruby with pride. There was a startled cry: 'Oh, Mother, look what she has done!' Her mother took the drawing and there was a spiteful gleam in her eye as she inspected it and asked: 'Do you consider this a very kind portrait of your poor old aunt?

13

You really are a nasty little thing. I don't know what Aunt Flo will think when she sees this. She has always been so fond of you and is such a kindly old soul.' She handed the drawing to a woman sitting on her left and, although I saw her lips twitch, I ran out before the drawing could do a full circle of the room. The only consolation was that I had missed all that kissing.

The days went on and on and there was no letter from home, and it seemed as if they had forgotten me. Mother had promised to come and fetch me herself. In theory she liked to stay at Tower Hill, although when she got there she was always fussing to return home. They were kind to her in a patronizing way, but always saying things like: 'Poor old Dora, with all those great children,' or 'Do sit down while you have the chance to rest,' and to me, 'You must look after your little mother.' They made her sound like a child-bride. Although extremely thin and fragile-looking, Mother was a tall woman and she certainly never had to work hard, at least she didn't in those days. Sometimes she was carried away by an enthusiasm for jam-making or bottling fruit, but normally she led an easy life, hardly ever appearing in the morning before ten o'clock and resting for an hour or two in the afternoon. There were three resident servants and a governess to look after us younger children; we did not entertain much, and the only exercise she took was to wander round the garden, her face carefully shielded by a parasol. Mother was willing to be treated as an over-worked little woman while she stayed at Tower Hill, but the patronage irritated her. To be introduced to people as 'my poor niece Dora' wasn't very complimentary. At home she was treated like a princess by Father, who was considerably older than she was, by about twenty years. With all her children away I guessed she must be having a wonderful time and would not be in a hurry to become 'poor Dora'.

Although Ruby was spiteful to me in her mother's presence, she was not unpleasant when we were alone, in fact she was quite affectionate. She really longed for love. Sometimes she became over-friendly with one of the servants, but Aunt Lawrence soon put a stop to it. I can remember her starting a friendship with the vicar's pretty daughter and for some reason there was trouble about that. I think they were a dirty family and the vicar was too High Church. Little bells rang when they shouldn't, and I'm not sure there wasn't a smell of incense in the church. I thought it was lovely.

After Charles went to Brussels I sometimes went visiting with Ruby to cottages or family friends. She used to say: 'I'm just off to see a dear little baby with water on the brain.' I would imagine a baby with a sort of private aquarium on its head and be disappointed to see a large-headed, dull-looking child. Another time it would be a girl who had married her uncle. I think she was French and it turned out it wasn't a real uncle, but it seemed interesting until I saw her. Then there was the little boy who had swallowed a brick. 'Oh yes, Ruby, please take me to see him,' I entreated. So we went to his nursery and saw a small, solemn boy of about four. It seemed impossible that he could have swallowed a brick, his mouth wasn't large enough to get a quarter of a brick in. I asked the nurse. Yes, it was true, he had swallowed a brick over a year ago and it had never been seen again. It was years later that I learnt that it was a toy, wooden brick. Then there was the elderly-looking woman and her young daughter who had both had babies on the same day, which resulted in a delightfully complicated family relationship, an uncle two hours younger than his nephew. The proud mother and daughter paraded up and down the village with their babies on fine evenings, but Aunt Lawrence said it was disgusting.

15

One morning, when Grace and her father were out riding together, I amused myself burying some baby chickens who had died of something called 'the pip', according to the bailiff's wife. It wasn't that I liked burying the chickens so much, it was the wreaths I enjoyed making. I wove hay into small circles and entwined wild flowers into it. I was glad Grace was out of the way so that I could enjoy my childish pastime in peace. But not for long, because Ruby came bustling into the dairy garden. She enjoyed appearing to be busy because there was so little to fill her days. She was too nervous to ride; she would have been accused of wasting time if she read; her attempts at sewing were not too successful; and for some reason she was not allowed a dog of her own. I believe there were some rabbits somewhere that were supposed to belong to her, but I never saw them. This time she wanted me to go to the lower part of the village, near the church, where she had to deliver a note to an old general. I went on twisting clover into my wreath and told her I was busy. When I saw the hurt expression on her face I felt guilty. Then she brightened and added that if I would accompany her she would show me some marvellous chairs, in fact they were made of human skin. I could hardly believe this, but decided to risk it even if they turned out to be dolls' chairs. I packed the remaining dead chickens into a night-light box and put them on a shady wall to be buried later. Then I washed my hands in the bailiff's kitchen, smoothed my hair with my wet hands and set off with Ruby across the village green.

We walked down the hill and various elderly villagers said: 'Good morning, Miss Ruby,' and she stopped and talked to them in her nervous manner, laughing and stamping her feet a little and bringing out bright sayings she had picked up from the maids: 'Well, this won't make the baby a new frock.' 'Time waits for no man.' 'More haste, less speed,' and bustled off, jerking her arms as she walked – we used to call it 'Ruby, doing arms'. Just before we reached the church, we came to a high mud wall with large holes right through, so that you got little pictures of green grass and cows' legs. Then the wall changed to brick, but that was not in very good condition either and, when we came to where the gates should have been, there were only posts. The drive was quite short and the large house was built of crumbling red brick and the woodwork was bleached like old bones. An oldish man with one of the reddest faces I have ever seen was riding down the drive on a white horse and he couldn't have been mistaken for anything else than a general, with his fierce white moustache and brave blue eyes. I turned to Ruby and whispered: 'Now I have come all this way, I must go into the house and see those chairs,' but she was already handing the General the note. He took it in his strangely freckled hand and muttered a gruff 'thank you', but as he rode off he shouted: 'If you'd like to go to the house, my wife will be pleased to see you.' Ruby turned to me excitedly. 'Fancy that! No one has ever met his wife, she hardly ever comes to the place. Now I'll be able to tell Mother all about her. What a piece of luck!' And she fairly skipped up the drive.

We walked in through the open front door, and a stable boy, wearing a dirty apron, appeared from the kitchen, drying a cup on a greasy cloth. He nodded his head towards a door and said: 'She's in there,' and stumped back to the kitchen. The hall was very large and the amazing thing was that grass was growing between the paving stones, not everywhere, but in quite a lot of places. I was careful not to walk on it. The boy suddenly appeared again without the cloth and cup and knocked on the door he had indicated before. I said: 'Take care, you are spoiling the grass.' He looked at me scornfully and said gruffly: 'Don't talk soft,' and returned to the kitchen. We went into a dusty room where the sun,

17

streaming through the dirty windows, made a perfect Jacob's ladder. There was the General's wife rising from a leather armchair, and, although she must have been middle-aged, she was beautiful. She was the first woman I had ever seen wearing make-up, at least enough to show. Her huge brown eyes had darkened lids and her full lips were very red. She held her head rather tilted back, showing a lot of white neck. She smelt simply wonderful. Her voice was drawling and slightly amused and, when she sat down, she arranged her legs so that you could see how lovely they were. I tried to put my legs in the same position, but the socks and garters spoilt the effect. I don't know what she made of her visitors, but she could tell I was admiring her and soon produced a large box of chocolates, which she placed on a card-table near me. The box was round, which made it appear more luxurious. I only dared to take one, they looked too good for public eating. The General's wife was saying that she had come down for a few days to see how the old man was managing, but she didn't think she could stand more than another night of it. 'I have my own house in London and we go our various ways, but from time to time I try to help him. Really this house is beyond a joke. He would have it because of the stables, obstinate old fool.'

I listened to her with bated breath but managed not to have my mouth open like Ruby. All the same I was not going to be done out of the skin chairs and abruptly interrupted with: 'Could I see the chairs, please?'

She turned her heavily powdered face to Ruby. 'Chairs, chairs. What does the child mean?'

I had not liked to mention that she and her husband sat on chairs made of human skin, but Ruby had no such scruples and replied: 'Oh, she means the chairs in your hall, the ones your husband had covered with skin. I'm afraid she is a morbid little thing.' She giggled and bounced about on her rickety chair. 'Perhaps I shouldn't have mentioned them to her because of little pitchers having long ears. Oh dear!' And she bounced about again and covered her mouth with her limp white hand.

The General's wife looked at her as if she had never seen a nervous girl before and said crossly: 'Those frightful things! I didn't know he still had them, but I suppose they must be somewhere here; as you say, in the hall perhaps.' She elegantly rose from her old leather chair as if it had been a golden throne, and we scrambled to our feet and followed her into the hall. We walked down it to a part where no grass grew and there was a sort of dark alcove with the air of a dining-room about it. There was a long refectory table with three massive oak chairs placed either side. They were dark and churchified, and the backs and seats were covered in what appeared to be vellum, blackish and cracked in places. The General's wife looked at them ruefully and admitted that the chairs were covered in human skin.

'He brought them back with him after the Boer War, isn't it horrible? Five of them are black men's skins and one white. I believe if you look carefully you can see the difference. He used to adore them, silly old man.'

One chair certainly was lighter than the rest and I carefully sat on it, expecting something strange to happen; but it was exactly like sitting in any other uncomfortable chair. My bare arms touched the back and, remembering what it was made of, I stood up and wiped my arms with my handkerchief. With a feeling of awe I gazed at the chairs thinking of the poor skinless bodies buried somewhere in Africa. Did their souls ever come to see what had happened to their skins or had they forgotten all about them? How had the General brought the skins back? And did the workmen who covered the chairs know what gruesome work they were doing?

I emerged from my dazed state to hear Ruby saying: 'We must be going now,' and we turned towards the main hall, passing a dreary little room with the door open, which appeared to contain nothing except tin boxes, boots and an unmade camp-bed covered with army blankets and no sheets: the General's bedroom. 'The poor old dear!' his wife laughed. 'He thinks he is on a campaign or something. Isn't it all too too uncomfortable?' It certainly was.

At luncheon Ruby chattered away about our morning visit and for once her mother did not snub her or tell the parlour-maid to stop breathing so loudly. 'Do you mean to say that dirty old man sleeps without sheets?' she asked, the half-smile she usually wore slightly more of a smile. 'You say her face was simply coated in powder. How disgraceful to appear like that in the country! Such a bad example! I have always heard that she is a dreadful woman, although I believe she is well connected.'

Turning to me, she asked what I thought of 'those revolting chairs'. I said I thought them 'weirdly mysterious' and then looked at her out of the corner of my eye, because I knew she wouldn't like me saying that. I was planning to myself how I would describe the chairs to Father when I got home, but I was wasting my time, because I never saw him again. He died two days later.

Two

I w a s cleaning out the canaries' cages when they sent for
me. The parlour-maid who breathed heavily said I was wanted
immediately. There was no time to wash my hands, so they
smelt of caged birds. I walked beside her through the crimson-
carpeted hall, hoping that perhaps Mother had come to fetch
me, although I had received no letter. There was no sound
of voices coming through the drawing-room door and, when
I went in, Aunt Lawrence was standing with her back to the
window and for once there was no half-smile on her face.
Uncle Lawrence stood near her, but looked as if he was longing to get out of the room as quickly as possible. There they
stood, so still, as if they were having their photograph taken;
and I wondered if they had just had a great quarrel in some
way connected with me. I was amazed when Aunt Lawrence
slowly walked up to me and put her arm round my shoulder
and called me Francie as they did at home. She told me to
be a brave girl for Mother's sake, and I thought something
terrible must have happened to Mother's hands, and that was
why she hadn't written. Then she told me that Father was
dead – only she called it passing away, so that I didn't realize
what she meant at first. I gathered he had died very suddenly
without any pain just as he was leaving the breakfast-table.

Fortunately 'my poor little mother' was there, so he did not die alone. Aunt Lawrence said I was to look at it as a merciful release. She spoke in a different voice than she usually used and the words were different too. For some reason both my hands went up to my mouth and there was the smell of birds. I just stood there, thinking of Father lying dead and stiff on the flowered dining-room carpet and poor Mother not knowing what to do – she depended on him for everything, we all did. I couldn't imagine a world without him, it seemed impossible that it would go on, and there was Uncle Lawrence making nervous, throat-clearing noises and Aunt Lawrence being affectionate. I knew they were waiting for me to do something, cry perhaps, but I felt there was nothing to do except go home quickly while at least Mother and my sisters and brothers remained. At last I was able to say: 'Can I go home at once, please?'

They exchanged glances and I was told, 'Not just yet; after the funeral, darling,' and was led from the room by Aunt Lawrence.

I was put in the night nursery with the curtains drawn and told to lie down, although I wasn't tired, only sort of stunned. They left the door open and people kept coming to look at me. I remember how self-conscious and miserable I felt, lying there in that darkened room, listening to the sound of horses' hooves stamping in the stables and distant ducks quacking. They seemed such sad sounds. Sometimes I cried and sometimes I slept and, although I felt so wretched, I couldn't help feeling hungry – and guilty about it. I was only allowed to eat bread and milk, and it tasted even more slimy than usual in the darkness.

A few days later they buried Father. The Lawrences drove off in their motor-car with the brass fittings gleaming in the sun, but I wasn't allowed to go with them. I stood in the yard with Ruby, watching them drive away. Uncle Lawrence looked rather splendid in his funeral clothes, but black didn't suit Aunt Lawrence. It seemed impossible to connect a black funeral with Father – it was as if it were some other man they were burying and Father had only disappeared. Ruby was holding something behind her back and, when the car had slowly passed through the arched gateway, she said with her thin lips grinning: 'Here's something to cheer you up,' and thrust a framed photograph of my father in my face. It must have been taken years ago, because his hair and moustache appeared very dark and there seemed to be an awful lot of white waistcoat and a horrible false background of a waterfall. It was a common sort of caricature of Father and I ran away, screaming at the top of my voice, leaving a dismayed Ruby standing there among the startled grooms.

Two weeks after the funeral I was still at Tower Hill. They were quite kind to me and there were no more mattress jokes, but I felt utterly miserable. I received a short letter from Mother telling me to be a good girl and stay where I was until things were sorted out. I wondered what they were sorting out. Father's clothes perhaps. In the coach-house there was his huge old iron bicycle with the rusty bell on the cross-bar, guarding all our little bicycles. Gradually collecting dust, his shining boots and leggings must be waiting for him in the boot-room, and his pipes would be hanging on the pipe-rack above his armchair in the morning-room. There was his enormous desk, filled with papers except for one fascinating drawer containing faded family photographs covering the last fifty years. They must be sorting out his money too. I remembered that Grace had said Father would not be able to leave us much money, so perhaps we would be poor and our house would smell stuffy and musty like a cottage. I decided I should still love it, however much it smelt.

Grace's German governess returned. She was not a real German, but a Swiss-German with a long fat face and hair done up very high on her forehead, which made her heavy face appear even longer. When she found I was living in the house, she said she did not feel well enough to teach two children, so I was turned out of the schoolroom while lessons were in progress. I was thankful for this, except that it was difficult to escape the grown-ups. I didn't enjoy my little excursions with Ruby any more, because I was an exhibit. 'This is my poor little cousin. You remember Dora? Her little girl. Her father has just died, leaving a widow and six children. Yes, it was all very sudden. In the midst of life we are in death. Many a true word spoken in jest – well, it's hardly a jest, but you know what I mean.' Then she would do her nervous little stamping dance and we would be off until we met someone else and I would be exhibited again.

One morning she asked if I would like to meet a young widow and her little baby. I said: 'Not if the widow is crying.' Ruby smiled and said that Vanda, the widow, was very brave and pretty. Like most children I liked pretty people, so I trotted off with Ruby, only stipulating that we by-passed the village and walked through the fields. We had to walk on the edge because the grass was almost ready for mowing, very tall and gently moving in the wind. There were dog-roses growing on the hedges and, although I knew from experience that the petals nearly always fell when carried in my warm hands, I couldn't help picking a few. We came to a sunless narrow lane with high banks. There had not been any rain recently, but it was muddy and deeply rutted by cart-wheels. A little stream ran down one side and it smelt of peppermints because of a weed that was growing on its banks. The farm suddenly appeared round a slight bend, surprising because it was so large and unexpected. The actual house was even more decrepit than the General's, but the farm buildings looked prosperous enough. We walked round the side of the house and found the widow playing tennis

24

with a young man on the most cracked and bumpy hard tennis-court I have ever seen. She was wearing blue bedroom slippers because, as she explained later, she had no tennis shoes and no money to buy any. I thought having the courage to wear bedroom slippers on a tennis-court fearfully dashing and Vanda more than pretty, really beautiful. The game was finished and the young man dismissed with: 'You had better go home now, Peter. I'm sure your father's expecting you.'

'Oh no, he doesn't,' Peter brought out with a slight stammer. 'He isn't at home today.'

'Well, in that case your mother needs you. Be off, there's a dear boy, and perhaps I'll play tennis with you tomorrow.'

So Peter was dismissed and Vanda turned her lovely face to Ruby and said: 'I'm so glad you've come,' and said it as if she really meant it. She absent-mindedly handed me her tennis racquet and ran her fingers through her dark, silky hair. 'God, I'm hot. Let's go into the house, perhaps there's something to drink there . . . No, there isn't, but we could squeeze some of the baby's oranges if that wretched little nursemaid has left any.'

We went into the house together and I saw it was very similar to the General's, except that it was considerably smaller. There was the same sort of atmosphere, only more depressing. 'This place really is sinister,' Vanda remarked as we went through the cellar-like kitchens. 'It's like an ice-house on the warmest day. But I can't grumble when I'm allowed to live here rent-free. They only use the farm, and the house had been empty for years until my cousin let me have it, but they never come near the place, which suits me.'

We went down a passage which led to the front of the house. The wallpaper had come away from the walls and hung down in curling rolls above our heads. At the end of the passage there was a large hall and, although the sun was

25

streaming in through one of the windows, it appeared un-
utterably depressing and I was relieved when Vanda opened
the door of her sitting-room. The room must have been a
small library, because it was lined with empty bookshelves.
It was sparsely furnished with garden furniture and a roll-
top desk. There were a few bright cushions in the chairs, and
someone had started to paint the furniture a harsh blue, but
hadn't got very far except for the floor, which was covered
in blue paint in places, sometimes with newspaper stuck to
it. There was a strong smell of mice, which, Vanda explained,
came from the drawing-room, where stacks of corn were
stored. She said she could hear them scuttling about at night.
'I should bring some of the farmyard cats in, but they are
half-wild and I'm scared they may hurt the baby,' she said
as she went about the room collecting dirty glasses and cups.
Now she mentioned the baby I could hear one crying. It
was sort of blended in with the farm noises and not very
noticeable.

Ruby said: 'Isn't that little Jane crying?'

The mother replied dejectedly: 'I expect so. You see that
horrible girl from the village has left – she just walked out –
and there is no one to look after Jane. Do you know anything about babies, Ruby?' Ruby said she didn't, but when
we went into the garden and found the poor baby strapped
down in its pram, sopping wet and angrily cramming its
fist in its mouth when it was not screaming, she did say it
was obvious that the baby needed its nappy changing and
seemed hungry. We heated milk on a primus stove and between us we changed the soggy napkin and gave her her
bottle. Then she seemed content and Ruby held her in her
arms and patted her back to bring some wind up. Vanda,
looking at her in astonishment, cried: 'Oh, you are wonderful, Ruby! How well you manage her! Dear, dear Ruby,
please come back this afternoon and help me. I think another

26

girl is coming from the village tomorrow, otherwise I don't know how I will manage.'

We returned to the farm in the afternoon and Vanda said we were darlings. If only we could stay with Jane, it would give her time to ride her bicycle into the village to do some shopping. She stayed away about two hours and the only shopping in her basket was a packet of cigarettes and bread; but she was so affectionate and grateful to us that we went away spellbound and talked about Vanda for the rest of the day – at least we did when we were alone.

Ruby spent most of her spare time at the farm after that. Not for long, though, because when Aunt Lawrence discovered her daughter was being used as a nursemaid, she tried to put a stop to it, although it was making her so happy. It was extraordinary how happy Ruby was; she even looked better.

Vanda was the kind of girl who appeared fashionable, whatever she was wearing. The slight twist of a scarf, a cardigan worn over her shoulder or back to front, a little cap at the back of her head, colours that clashed – everything she wore appeared delightful, even a battered rainproof hat on a rainy day. Poor Ruby tried to imitate her, but clashing colours or a cardigan worn with buttons down the back just looked peculiar on her, as her mother repeatedly pointed out, and reluctantly she returned to her bulky tweeds with the skirts hanging down more at the back than the front or, on warm days, the dreary poplin dresses with buttons all over them and limp collars. She wore a black band on her arm for my father. No one else did, but she liked people to ask who she was mourning for. They had put a black bow on my hair and someone, probably Old Nanny, had brought me long black socks, otherwise I still wore my usual cotton dresses. Aunt Lawrence did once produce a frightful black felt hat which Aunt Flo had left behind years ago. She stuck

27

it on my head and said I wasn't to go outside without it. It was so large that it covered my eyes and most of my nose and it smelt of old ladies. Then she pinned it back in some way so that it stuck on the top of my head like a top hat. I longed to say: 'Would you like Grace to go about like this?' but was too afraid, so I bawled instead, which turned out to be the best thing I could have done because it disturbed Uncle Lawrence, who opened the door a chink, looked into the hall where the noise was coming from, and said in his charming voice: 'Take that appalling thing off the child's head,' and closed the door. That was the end of Aunt Flo's hat, although I'm sure if Vanda had put it on her head it would have appeared a delightful sort of hat, perhaps even started a new fashion.

Ruby crept off to the farm whenever she could escape her mother's hard blue eye. Sometimes I accompanied her. There was a nursemaid now, but she knew almost as little about babies as Vanda, and Jane really depended on Ruby, who appeared to know quite a lot about baby-feeding. I had been five years old when my brother Toby was born and I only had vague memories of what went on in the nursery at that time, but I did remember seeing him splashing about in a little bath every morning and being fed on bottles of warm milk at frequent intervals. Jane's meals seemed to consist of cups or bottles of cold milk and very dirty bread and butter. If the sun was shining, an enamel bowl was placed in the garden and, when the sun had warmed it a little, Jane had her bath on the lawn. If there was no sun, there was no bath. Someone with fairly modern ideas must have instilled into Vanda's head that babies needed orange juice, because she often asked the dim-witted nursemaid if she had given the baby its orange juice. If anyone remarked that Jane seemed rather unfortunate and neglected, Vanda would appear quite hurt and say: 'Well, I'm only twenty-four; what can you expect?' And then add brightly, 'But she has her orange juice.'

I had never been interested in babies, but with Jane it was different. As soon as she saw me, she would hold up her funny little arms and make queer noises to show she wanted to be lifted. If I had her on my lap, she would cling to my dress and refuse to be taken away, and, although she was not pretty, when she was not crying with hunger or indigestion she was a cheerful child, and I have never seen anyone so young laugh the way she laughed. She must have been about eight months old when I first saw her, looking younger because she was so small. Her large brown eyes were full of humour and intelligence, but her mouth had a sort of bruised look.

I used to think Vanda was not pleased to see us when her friend the Major was there and tried to explain this to Ruby, but she did not agree and said Vanda would be more pleased to see us than usual because we were chaperones. All the same, I kept out of the way when he was about – I could usually tell when he was there because I could see his car standing outside the house. It was rather a special one with a name like Talbot-Darracq and he was immensely proud of it. When I saw it there, I would turn away and let Ruby go in alone. The Major's face was very red and his big, bold eyes very blue, and he smelt of drink and hair-oil. He paid Ruby elaborate compliments and called her his 'little jewel', and, although I knew he was making fun of her and found it embarrassing, she enjoyed it.

Now the governess had returned, I had to share Grace's bedroom. It had once been the old night nursery and in spite of its dark green walls it had a cosy look. We were allowed a night-light, because several times during the night I had disturbed the house by screaming fits caused by nightmares. They may have been caused by the shock of Father's death, for I had never suffered from them before. One night I dreamt that Mother's head had been severed and made into a pork pie. Although it was a pork pie, I could still see it was a dead head. There was another fearful dream that Father was floating down the canal, all enlarged with water, and that eels were living in him. Now that there was a night-light, I did not cry for long when I woke up after one of these frightful dreams, but I dared not go to sleep again in case another came. To keep myself awake and to calm myself I would go through each room at home so that it almost seemed as if I was there. I tried to recall everything they contained: the yellow rug in the drawing-room, which we used to cut pieces from to make dolls' wigs; the faded morning-room curtains with monkeys climbing up them – it was always a sign that summer was coming when they were hung; the enormous brass bedstead in the spare room, all draped in chintz curtains, with its feather mattress – sometimes we slept there when we were ill, because it was on the sunny side of the house, and Father used to thump the mattress to make a hollow for us to lie in. There was a queer brass rail edging the step which led to the lavatory, and outside it hung the picture of a young woman with her mouth slightly open, surrounded by cupids, a dance programme in her hand. The smaller the detail I could remember, the happier I felt – which of the doors that led from the kitchen had latches and which had handles, for instance. Once a guinea-pig had died in the kitchen and one of the maids had held a small mirror to its mouth to see if its breath left a mark, and ever after I seemed to see the mark of the guinea-pig's last breath on it. I would think of home with such concentration that it seemed as if my spirit had left my body and I was really there.

It had been early in May when I first arrived at Tower Hill and now it was the middle of June and they were making the hay, taking advantage of the exceptionally fine weather. Grace and I were allowed to picnic in the fields one afternoon, but it wasn't the same without any young children to make houses for. The hay didn't even smell as strong as it did at home. It was the day we had the picnic that Uncle and Aunt Lawrence were talking about a sale which they were attending somewhere miles away. When they saw that I was listening, Uncle Lawrence said: 'Not before the child.' I knew they sometimes went to horse sales, at least my uncle did, so I couldn't understand why they wanted to make a secret of it. I had a wild idea that they were going to buy me a pony of my own, a white one complete with new harness. Although I knew this was extremely unlikely, I comforted myself with the thought all day.

When we were haymaking in the field, Grace suddenly put down her fork and said: 'I know something you don't know,' and she jumped backwards and forwards over the haycock, rolling her eyes and laughing. Then she asked what I liked best at home, what was my favourite thing. I said: 'Everything.' She shook her head at me and laughed again for some silly reason of her own. The governess told her to behave herself, but she went on giggling until she was distracted by finding a poor frog that had had its legs severed by the mower.

At last Mother was coming to Tower Hill. They didn't say anything about me going home, but surely Mother couldn't return without me? I was longing to see her, but at the same time a little afraid in case she had altered now that she had become a widow. I couldn't bear to think that her hair had suddenly turned white or that she had taken to wearing spectacles; even to picture her dressed in black was upsetting. It was difficult to imagine how she would manage the journey without Father to drive her to the station and buy her railway ticket. He even used to help her pack, airing the trunks and suitcases on the veranda the previous day. I told Old Nanny that I was going home and asked her if I could do my own packing, but she dismayed me by saying that I was not leaving immediately; my mother had enough worries as it was, without me adding to them. She stood there in her crumbling whiteness like some old angel demanding obedience and I dared not even cry until she left the room. I could hardly believe Mother could be so heartless as to leave me pining away at Tower Hill when once she knew how I hated being there. Surely she would relent and take me back with her? Although she became tired of her children sometimes, she always wanted us home in the end and gave us a tremendous welcome on our return.

My uncle owned a motor-car and chauffeur, but it was only used for long journeys and special occasions, except when Charles drove it when he was at home. On the morning that Mother was expected there was some discussion whether she should be met at the station in the dog-cart or the car. 'Poor thing,' they decided. 'We must make a special occasion of it and meet her in the Napier with little Frances, just Frances and no one else.' It was thought more fitting that I should meet my widowed mother alone. Feeling proud, I sat back against the light grey upholstery with my arm through a hanging strap and my black legs neatly folded. Then I was standing on the station platform in a howling wind; it was that sort of station. As I waited with my cotton dress flapping against my legs, I became more and more embarrassed at the thought of seeing Mother again. Would I be smothered in black arms and tears and would she be bent with care and poorly dressed with a widow's bugled bonnet on her head and soiled gloves on her hands? Most of the widows I had met wore perpetual black and took to an ear-trumpet. But I remembered Vanda and felt reassured, and a minute or two later the train steamed in and there was Mother stepping from the train and being handed her luggage by a handsome, silver-haired man. She was smiling her thanks and appeared exactly the same as usual, wearing a pretty black and white dress she had sometimes worn for summer bridge parties. She gave me a quick kiss, no smothering hug; then her face suddenly crumpled and she said: 'Oh darling, such dreadful things have been happening since I saw you last. Everyone has been so kind, but I can't think how I'm going to manage. So many decisions to make, and people are inclined to rush one so. If only I could have a little more time to decide what to do for the best.' She vaguely looked round the platform and asked in a disappointed voice: 'Didn't anyone else come to meet me?' I explained that they had sent the car to meet her and that they had all wanted to come to the station, but thought she would prefer to see me alone. I was rather apologetic about this. As soon as we were sitting in the car she exclaimed: 'The pony's gone and the trap, so I have no idea how we will get about in future. The Winnets bought her. Poor Belinda will be a baker's pony now.' I said that we would be able to manage with our bicycles, then remembered that Mother couldn't ride one. So poor little Belinda had gone. I remembered how patient she had been when we took turns to ride her: she was such a gentle creature that even Mother used to drive her in the trap. I supposed this is what they meant by 'sorting out' – selling Belinda, and what other treasured possessions? I dared not ask, because I felt it was better to last a little longer without knowing.

In spite of all that Mother had been through, she was certainly looking very pretty. Her heavy-lidded eyes were still as large and blue as ever and her fragile pink and white face was completely unlined. Everything about her was delicately soft – soft skin, soft golden-brown hair and gently sloping shoulders – and the expression on her face was soft and vague, her eyes a little unfocused and her lips slightly parted. No wonder Father had loved and spoilt her so much.

We were driving along a tree-lined piece of road called the Straight Mile and on our right there was a new building estate composed of small villas and short roads. The houses were built very close to each other and where the estate ended there were flat, empty-looking fields. Mother eyed the estate with distaste and remarked that they were enough to make her grandfather turn in his grave. There were so many other people sharing Great-grandfather's grave that I said he had not much room to turn in; but I could see by Mother's face that this remark displeased her, so I asked if Polly and John were at home or if they had returned to school. They had both come home for Father's funeral. Mother's face did not clear and she said: 'Yes, John is back at Malvern, but Polly is at home and is being most helpful.' There was a pause before she added in a low voice as if to herself: 'But she is a little overbearing.'

We drove into the village in silence; but as the brick face of Tower Hill appeared before us, Mother sighed: 'Oh, how glad I am to be away from all those lot numbers and the utter heartbreak of it all,' and I knew that, as soon as she saw her uncle and aunt, there would be tears.

The tears were over and so was luncheon and now all the grown-ups had gathered in the drawing-room to discuss poor Dora's future. It did not look as if it would be a bright one from the expression on their faces and, when they came out, I could see that Mother had been crying again. Aunt Lawrence saw me hanging about the door and called me to her. Mother had gone upstairs to repair the damage done to her face, so I followed Aunt Lawrence into the drawing-room, where she started banging the cushions about to make them a proper shape after people had been squashing them. As she bent over the cushions, she told me I was to be a sensible girl and cheer my poor mother up and help her to meet certain changes that must take place. 'You see, your father has not left her at all well-off – very remiss of him, but I for one always expected it. Your mother will have to cut her coat according

34

to her cloth in future and she will find it very hard. Now, for instance, this afternoon we are taking her to see a small house. It is only a few minutes away, so we would be able to keep an eye on her; but, although it is quite a convenient sort of place and is well enough in its way, it is not the sort of home she is used to. Well, Frances, I want you to tell her how much you like it and how happy you all will be there, and I'm sure you will be happy there. It is easy for young people to make changes and often does them a world of good.'

I asked in amazement why we couldn't go on living at home; after all it was our own freehold house. She told me we could not afford the upkeep of a great place like that. Unfortunately it could not be sold for some years because it became John's property when he came of age; but in the meantime, if it was let advantageously, it would bring in something towards his school fees. She appeared annoyed that the house could not be sold, but I found it a great consolation. Everything that I loved seemed to be disappearing so rapidly.

We went to see the house – Mother, Aunt Lawrence, Ruby, Grace and I. We walked and the horrid little Floss came barking and frisking round our legs. We crossed the village green and turned to the left, and I began to have a sinking feeling. I looked at Mother, but she was absent-mindedly nodding to the village women who were standing at their doors, trying to get a glimpse of the new widow. She whispered: 'I can feel their eyes boring into the white parts of my dress.' We came to the Straight Mile and still she had not noticed where we were going; she just trailed along under the trees, not listening to Aunt Lawrence's bracing remarks. Suddenly she almost tottered back on her high heels and cried: 'Surely you are not taking me to that dreadful building estate! I couldn't live there, you can't expect me to.' Her voice had risen to a wail and she just stood there in the road, not walking any more. Aunt Lawrence took her arm and somehow managed to make her move, gently murmuring soothing words as she propelled her forward: 'Dear Dora, you know how much your happiness means to us. We want to do all we can to help you, but it is very difficult when you have been left so badly off. The actual house we are going to see has been built for the last twenty years, although I admit it is surrounded by new houses – and very convenient some of them are, I believe. They are snapped up immediately by the Howlet Engineering people, so it was impossible to obtain one for you. This house I want you to consider – The Hollies, I think it is called, such a cheerful name – it only became vacant a few days ago and we have a twenty-four-hour option. We were really very fortunate to get it.'

After a lot of persuasion, Mother reluctantly inspected The Hollies. It was built of dark red and yellowish bricks, more yellow ones than red. It had a slate roof and two dormer windows upstairs, like a cat's ears sticking up. There were two square, sunless reception-rooms either side of the passage, and upstairs there were four square bedrooms. The bathroom was downstairs, next to the kitchen. The kitchen was the most attractive room in the house, with french windows leading into the garden, a large dresser and an Eagle range – though just now it was smelling of paraffin and blown-out candles. Mother was very quiet, walking through the rooms and ignoring her aunt's over-enthusiastic comments. Ruby was hopping about from one foot to the other, exclaiming in a bossy voice: 'You won't be able to have rooms of your own any more. You'll all have to share. It will be such a squash, but you'll be as snug as bugs in a rug.' I asked where the maids would sleep. 'Maids!' Aunt Lawrence snorted. 'It will be a gross extravagance if you occasionally have a woman in to help. You three elder girls will have to work for a change. For instance, you could be the parlourmaid, Polly the cook and Esmé the housemaid.' Grace chimed in with: 'Oh Mother, will they wear uniforms and call me Miss Grace when I come to the house?'

I shouted: 'Children can't be maids! There's a law about it, because they have to go to school.'

Grace gave her mother a sly glance and muttered: 'Board school. That's where you'll go.'

I rushed at her and started to pummel her with my fists until I was gripped by one arm and firmly dragged away by Aunt Lawrence. 'How can you behave like this when your father's hardly cold in his grave?' she hissed as she twisted my arm. How I hated all this talk about graves! I turned to Mother, hoping she would come to my defence, but she was staring out of the window at the creosoted fence which surrounded the garden. It ended in a sharp point where a piece had been cut off to make a new road, and, although it was June, there was not a single flower blooming.

Aunt Lawrence became all brisk: 'You two children, kiss and make up. I can't have you fighting like this.' And she stood over us like a schoolmistress until we eventually did kiss, although it caused us both embarrassment and ended in my having frightful hiccupy giggles. I was still suffering from them when Aunt Lawrence firmly locked the front door and pointed to the dusty holly hedge: 'Look at this nice hedge. It will give you some privacy and think how charming it will look when it is covered in red berries, so useful for Christmas decoration.'

Three

WITHIN three weeks we were established in The Hollies
– Mother, Polly and I, little Clare, who had been born with
a hand missing, and Toby, who was only four. John was
still at boarding school and so was Esmé, the sister nearest
to me in age. There was no maid, but we did have a daily
help, even if it was 'gross extravagance'. I stayed on at Tower
Hill until the family moved in and, except for Ruby, I think
they were getting pretty tired of having me around. On the
whole, I didn't behave badly, but I was too young to fit in
and they must have found it a nuisance having me at the
luncheon table day after day. I had not paid any more visits
to the General, but saw Vanda and her baby frequently. I
visited her one afternoon when she wasn't expecting me.
Grace was out riding with her father, Ruby was paying
formal calls with her mother, and I was supposed to be
amusing myself grooming the yard dogs, Dobbs and Dash. I
discovered some horrible creatures like small ticks on them
and didn't like to touch them after that, so went round the
yard stroking the soft nose of any horse that had its head
hanging over a door. Some of the grooms were sitting on low
chairs and upturned buckets round the saddle-room door and
they asked me if I had a pony of my own at home. After I'd
told them about Belinda becoming a baker's pony, I felt

slightly depressed and left them and wandered round the paddock looking for four-leaved clovers. Then I found I was walking through the fields towards Vanda's farm, although I had no previous intention of going there. I hoped she would be pleased to see me and have something useful for me to do: dress Jane and take her out in the pram or go to the village to buy cigarettes. There was usually a mass of things she needed doing and I was bored with my aimless afternoon. There was no sign of Jane when I arrived and I remembered there was another new nursemaid who must be pushing her about somewhere, but there might be some shopping I could do. I walked into the house and called Vanda, but, as there was no answer, I looked through the half-opened door of the room she used as a sitting-room. Vanda was asleep in a deck-chair and I stood hesitating by the door, not knowing what to do. Then I went into the room and stood close to her. She didn't move. She was lying in the deck-chair and for once she wasn't looking beautiful. Her face appeared almost coarse, her mouth was a little open and she was slightly snoring. There was a peculiar smell in the room, and I had an instinctive feeling that something was wrong. I noticed that there was an opened telegram on an ink-stained card-table and wondered if it contained bad news. There was a used glass and a bottle of sherry there too and a wasp was hovering over the glass. I stood vaguely worrying in case the wasp stung Vanda; on the other hand, if I bashed it with something it might wake her up and would certainly break the glass. As I meditated what to do, I suddenly became afraid: afraid of the sleeping Vanda and the dirty room with the sun beating in through the closed windows, of the smell and the wasp. There was something bad about the place. I turned away and left her to the mercies of the wasp, which was now behaving quite well and drinking from the glass. Soon it would become drunk, and I had a horrible suspicion that Vanda was drunk too. I'd frequently seen drunken men singing sad songs and walking crookedly, but there was something extra frightening about a drunken woman.

When I was alone with Ruby after tea, I told her about my visit to Vanda, just saying something seemed wrong with her and that I thought she might be ill. I didn't say what my suspicions were. Ruby managed to slip away while her mother went round to the bailiff's wife to complain that she had put too much salt in the butter. The bailiff's wife was always getting into trouble. The previous week there was trouble because Aunt Lawrence had seen her sixteen-year-old daughter riding a bicycle accompanied by a young man. As soon as her mother's back was turned, Ruby hurried away through the fields and managed to return before her absence was noticed. She said that she had found Vanda in bed, very unwell and unhappy because the Major had failed to arrive when it had been arranged that he would spend the day with her. She had booked a table at the Red Lion on his instructions and was waiting for him when the telegram arrived saying he was not coming after all. He was unavoidably detained; that was all he said. Ruby told me that the shock and disappointment had made Vanda quite sick and dazed and she seemed to hardly know what she was saying. 'I couldn't hear very distinctly, but she seemed to be talking about the most extraordinary things,' Ruby said with her brow all puckered.

I met Vanda in the village a few days later and her lovely little face looked as enchanting as ever. She was riding her bicycle and dismounted when she saw me and showed me a baby bird she had found on the road. Although it hadn't a red breast, she said it was a young robin and she was taking it home to see if she could rear it. It seemed ridiculous that I had been afraid of her.

I left Tower Hill the day the family moved into The Hollies. After thanking Aunt Lawrence for having me I just walked away, and one of the farm men brought my luggage round later. It was wonderful to be walking home, even if it was a different home to the one I had been used to. Life at The Hollies was quite different to anything I had experienced before and the thing I found most difficult to get used to was seeing Mother in a strange setting, busy in the kitchen cooking mutton, dressed in a huge white apron which she had discovered somewhere. It may have belonged to the Lawrences' nanny. Sometimes she would dab at the furniture with a yellow duster, gazing with triumph at the few good pieces we had managed to keep. She never went shopping, although she ordered meat when the butcher called at the house (the fishmonger soon stopped calling because he said it wasn't worth it when we always ordered herrings), and I think she would have considered it the final degradation to have been seen carrying a shopping-basket. Polly was the mainstay of the family; she organized us in an almost savage way. She was the first to get up in the morning, calling us on her way down to the kitchen. It was she who lit the range and prepared the breakfast. I had to dress myself and the two children, at least supervise them because they wouldn't let me help them. Clare took ages struggling with buttons with only one hand, singing to herself all the time; Toby kept putting his clothes on back to front and sometimes both legs through one trouser-leg, but he would do it himself. By the time we clattered downstairs the kettle was boiling and the oatmeal porridge, which had been made the previous night, was warming up. Polly only allowed us to eat bacon on Sunday morning and then it was striped, not pink. There she would be, rattling knives out of the knife-box, taking china off the dresser, her bushy fair hair tied back with a stiff black bow and her large, handsome face full of purpose.

41

She was a well-built girl, with rosy cheeks and rather a heavy profile. A strange thing about her face was the fact that her eyes, which had Mother's heavy lids, were set so that they slanted downwards away from her nose. This gave an interest to what would have otherwise been a too wholesome face. She appeared older than her fifteen years and her character had developed in the few weeks after Father's death. She had always been inclined to manage us; now she was in her element and we had all become a little afraid of her. When she left the house to shop or for some useful purpose, we immediately relaxed. I would take up a book which I kept hidden under the cushion of the wickerwork kitchen chair; Clare would play her mouth-organ. She didn't just make a noise, she played real tunes. Toby usually managed to eat something, because he wasn't allowed to eat between meals when Polly was around. Mother would sit in a chair in the square drawing-room or wander round the garden. The only things that grew there were golden rod, michaelmas daisies and the silver skeletons of honesty. There was a tall sycamore tree which Uncle Lawrence said should be cut down. Although it was not beautiful, it was our only tree, and the home and resting-place of many birds.

During the afternoon Polly would endeavour to teach the little ones, and it would be my chance to escape. Sometimes Ruby would call for me and we would walk together to Vanda's. She was again without a nursemaid, so we would try and help with the baby. Ruby had even bought a book on rearing babies, but she had to keep it hidden from her mother. When Vanda saw us coming through the tangled garden, she would explain: 'Oh, my dears! How lovely to see you! Would you be perfectly sweet and mind Jane while I rush round on my bicycle and pay a few bills? I've been chained to the house.' Of course we were sweet, and she would dash off, sometimes not returning for several hours,

Ruby becoming hurt and worried after the first hour and in a panic about her mother by the second. It often ended in me being left to mind the baby by myself. When Vanda did return, she was in high spirits and would tell me about some amusing man she had met, someone she hadn't seen for simply ages, and he had insisted that she had tea with him in the Red Lion. She talked to me about her men friends as if I was grown up, and I found this fascinating.

Quite near to Vanda's farm, I discovered a ruined barn with the mud walls that appealed to me so much. A rickety ladder made from wood with the bark still on it led up to the loft, and I liked to sit up there reading and eating plums or any odds and ends of fruit I'd been able to smuggle from the house. I'd taken two wooden boxes I'd found below and used them as a chair and table. The chair was also a book-case and contained several *Little Folks* and *Chatterbox* annuals and two books that Mother had had as a girl, *The Dove in the Eagle's Nest* and *Wide, Wide World*. I liked to cry over the last one. I usually decorated the table with wild flowers in a fish-paste jar, and inside the table I kept a few egg-cups which had once contained Easter eggs, and some Japanese cups. Often I would just sit on my box chair thinking and looking out of the window, which was really a squarish hole in the wall. I very much wanted a broom to sweep the floor, which was littered with straw, and I thought a small rug would make it look more furnished. If only I could find one that no one wanted. At first I'd been afraid to leave my things there, but when nobody ever appeared near the place, I lost my fear. I did not mention my loft to the family, but thought I might share it with Esmé when she returned for the holidays.

It had been arranged by Aunt Lawrence that we were to attend a girls' high school in the autumn. It was situated in the nearest town, which was about three miles away, and when I asked how Esmé and I were to get there, now that our bicycles had been sold, she said it would be good for us to walk. I dreaded the idea of school, partly because I had met very few girls of my own age, and also I had a premonition, which later proved only too true, that I was backward. Miss Grove, our last governess, was not a brilliant teacher and had only become a governess because her father had gone bankrupt, and we were her first pupils. Our governesses had changed pretty frequently, because Mother soon became weary of having them around. She said they always talked about their fathers or brothers or both. During breakfast they would say: 'My father always eats two Blenheim apples before breakfast', or 'My brother will only eat Cooper's Oxford marmalade', and at luncheon, 'My father always insisted on the plates being really warm,' or 'My brother never eats twice-cooked meat.' Mother once burst out with: 'Your brother sounds a very greedy man,' and that was the end of that governess.

I was to have been sent to the school where Polly and Esmé boarded, when Polly left. Father had explained that he could not afford to have more than two girls at school at the same time. He liked to discuss things with us, and when he made a new will a year or two before he died, he mentioned to us that he had left Clare £500 because she was handicapped and would need special training if ever it became necessary for her to earn her own living. I was only seven or eight at the time, but I can remember how we four elder ones sat with Father round the morning-room table discussing Clare's problem, and how we all agreed that she should have special mention in his will, although I hadn't a clear idea of what a will was at the time. Another day we sat round the table with a very different problem. Would it be kinder to have old Jimmy, our Yorkshire terrier, put to sleep by a vet or let him continue his suffering old age? I

44

was all for him continuing his suffering, but was outweighed by the rest of the family, who agreed that, swollen, deaf and sore-eyed, he should end his life. The following day we were taken for a picnic in the bluebell woods, and when we returned old Jimmy had gone.

Now we were living at The Hollies, it had become customary for Mother and one of us children to have Sunday luncheon at the Lawrences. Polly always stayed at home to cook for whoever remained, but I don't think she minded, because she didn't get on very well with Aunt Lawrence. On the way to Tower Hill, Mother would say: 'You will behave well, won't you, dear? It is so kind of them to have us every Sunday like this, and I do enjoy being waited on for a change.' But on the way back it would be a different story. 'When they bought the Crown Derby dinner service in the sale, I thought they had bought it for me and even thanked them, and now they are using it. It is so cruel to have it on the table when I'm there to see it. Did you hear how old Lady Scoby was admiring it? I longed to say it was mine,' or, 'I'm afraid Aunt Lawrence is sometimes very snubbing to me now we are poor,' or, rather wistfully: 'They always give us the chicken's legs.'

We had to be grateful to the Lawrences all the time, although all they had done was find us a horrible cheap house and give us Sunday luncheons for not more than two, and occasionally an odd rabbit or some pigeons. I couldn't bear seeing Mother being so grateful, but the Lawrences were the only relations she had. It must have been a terrible shock to her to suddenly find herself responsible for six children on an income of about three hundred a year from shares in the despised mattress factory. Uncle Frederick had paid for his brother's funeral expenses and was providing a cross made of Cornish granite for his grave, but had made it quite clear that was the only help he was giving. He was an elderly retired Civil Servant with a square, youngish wife with a heavy chin. There had been a tentative offer to adopt Toby, but of course we couldn't part with him. Now that she was alone, Mother had come to depend on us more, and as the days slowly passed she would often mention how much she was looking forward to having John and Esmé home for the holidays. She would start worrying in case The Hollies would be a shock to them. 'If only we could have new wallpaper in the rooms,' she would say sadly as she looked at the dining-room and drawing-room walls decorated with dark green things which may have been cabbages and marked by other people's pictures. 'Those green things are dreadfully depressing. How I wish we could have silver striped paper as we had at home.' She did mention to the Lawrences that she was considering having the main rooms re-papered, but they said it was out of the question, she couldn't possibly afford such a wanton extravagance. Then Polly had the bright idea of distemper, which was not common in those days except for nurseries and kitchens. Our daily woman said her husband was 'a dab hand with a brush'. He was called Hand, and he really was a handy man. For a very small sum he completely transformed the two box-like rooms. We chose a pale shade of yellow to give an illusion of the sun that never shone on that side of the house, and it was extraordinary the difference it made. Our few pieces of good furniture looked lovely without the ugly background of cabbages. Aunt Lawrence grudgingly admitted the improvement and even went as far as to say Mother was turning into a sensible little woman.

The primrose walls were a small thing in themselves, but from that time Mother became more cheerful and interested in her daily life. I think she found Polly a trial, but she would have never been able to manage without her. She had always been interested in cooking but, except for preserving fruit and jam-making and birthday cakes or dishes for special occasions, she had only supervised the cooking before. Now, in her big apron, she was beginning to enjoy herself, experimenting with puff pastry, cakes, savouries and soups. Mrs Hand prepared the vegetables and we washed up, so she had none of the drudgery. Delicious iced cakes appeared on the table at tea-time, *vol-au-vent*, lobster croquettes and chicken soufflés at midday and savoury supper in the evening. The little ones became bilious and, when Polly discovered that we had spent nearly a month's supply of money in a week, we went back to stews and rice-puddings, fish-pie and baked apples. But Mother had her way about the cakes and an occasional exotic pudding.

As July went on, we had great discussions about how the bedrooms were to be allotted when the rest of the family came home. It always boiled down to Mother, Polly and John each having a room to themselves and the rest of the family all being huddled into one room. Eventually Mother agreed to have Toby in her bedroom if Polly had Clare; then Esmé and I could share and John have a room to himself. This was considered important. Nothing was good enough for John: we all adored him and were convinced he was the most handsome, clever, noble boy in the world, and so he was. We had a shelf put up in his room for his books and displayed his two beloved guns. There was Father's double-barrelled one to add to the collection now. His clothes were unpacked from the trunks where they had been stored with mothballs, and brushed and pressed and hung in the wardrobe, although they were mostly winter ones and not needed until next term. A large oak writing-table and an armchair were lugged upstairs, in case he wanted to study, but still we considered the room did not look manly enough for a boy of fourteen. A cut-glass whisky decanter was suggested, but this was considered not quite suitable and we substituted

47

a heavy silver inkstand. Suddenly we remembered the lion-skin rug entombed in the dining-room chest, and it was taken out and placed over the threadbare carpet, its one-eyed head facing the door and its savage, almost toothless, jaws snarling. This, we felt, completed the room, although Mother said wistfully: 'What a pity he is too young to smoke! It just needs a tobacco-jar or, if he was taking up medicine, a skull.'

John and Esmé arrived home the same day. Mother was expecting the Lawrences to offer the use of their car or pony-trap, but the suggestion was never made and she had to hire a cab twice in one day. The hall was filled with corded trunks and boxes and excited voices. Esmé had brought a cage of white mice home with her and John was wearing another boy's shoes he had won in a dormitory raffle the previous evening. They both said the house was not as bad as they expected, and they both wanted to know what there was to eat because they were starving. When Esmé saw our bedroom she said: 'Bags I the bed by the window.' It made me feel shy of her when she used schoolgirl expressions, but I agreed that she should have first choice of beds because she was the eldest, and we changed the sheets over, as mine were already half dirty. For the first day or two I was still a little scared of her, then she stopped being a school-girl and became Esmé, completely unaffected, fearless and generous. She was three years older than I and was John's constant companion, a position we all envied. He taught her how to shoot and swim, and she was the only girl in the family who rode well. She wore her straight, almost black hair short in a fringe over her shining eyes, which had extra-ordinarily thick lashes. Her skin was sallow and her mouth large, her lips slightly brownish and her teeth very white. She was almost plain, and she was almost beautiful; even the people who called her plain could not keep their eyes away from her mobile, lively face. Polly found it difficult to

48

manage her. If Esmé raided the larder and came out eating a great hunk of bread or cold pie, she turned away pretending not to notice, but if I tried to do the same I was dragged out of the larder by one arm and told I was a greedy-guts. Then Esmé would wink one of her enormous eyes, which indicated that I was to follow her and share whatever she had taken. She would shuffle down late for breakfast, wearing a crimson dressing-gown and bedroom slippers, and exclaim: 'Have you almost finished? What heaven it is to get up late!' Then Mother started to follow suit and came down a little later each morning, trying to avoid Polly's reproachful eye as she made herself fresh tea and toast. When her lateness became an established habit, Polly suddenly pounced on her as she was creeping into the dining-room. 'Really, Mother!' she exclaimed crossly. 'If you find it so difficult to get up in the morning, it would be more economical if I carried your breakfast up to your room. At least it would save making a fresh pot of tea.' John laid down the apple he was cutting into funny shapes for Toby, stared at her in astonishment and said: 'Polly, you can't speak to Mother like that, she is entitled to do whatever she likes.' Polly went very red and her lower lip seemed to swell. As she loaded the used porridge-bowls on to a tray she muttered: 'I don't expect you realize how much tea costs.' Mother stood quite still with the objectionable pot of tea in her hands, looking at us as if we were strangers, then slowly placed the pot on the table and left the room. She stayed upstairs for most of the morning mending clothes and was quieter than usual for the rest of the day, but after that she came down to breakfast promptly, leading a neatly dressed Toby by the hand.

John and Esmé said the Lawrences couldn't be so mean as not to let them ride their horses occasionally, so after a few days, when no offer of a mount had materialized, they went

49

round to Tower Hill to do what they called 'stirring up their generous impulses'. They hung about the farm all morning and eventually asked Uncle Lawrence if they could help with the exercising some mornings. 'I'd rub the horses down and help a bit too,' John added. But Uncle Lawrence replied coldly: 'We have sufficient grooms for that sort of work, and I'm afraid my horses are far too valuable to let you and your sister ruin their mouths, or worse.' John spluttered: 'But you used to let us ride your horses, Uncle, and you always said how well Esmé rode. Rory and Tarquin and the bay mare Cherry – you used to let us ride them and we never did them any harm.' Uncle Lawrence drawled that he had no remembrance of lending his horses to children unless it was some old hack, but there was nothing like that in the stables now. He turned away and walked deliberately towards the house and the privacy of his study.

When he had gone, one of the grooms, who had been listening, said it was a shame and what a pleasure it was to see Miss Esmé ride. There was a little fifteen-hand mare in the stables eating its head off, it was just right for Miss Esmé. It had been bought as a second mount for Miss Grace, but she had taken a dislike to it after a little trouble concerning a steam-roller.

John and Esmé were furious when they returned home and told us all this, and they refused to go to the Lawrences' Sunday luncheon the following day. They had been specially invited and Mother did everything she could to make them change their minds, even resorting to tears, but they remained firm. John said that, if he was invited, perhaps he would go another Sunday, but he must wait until his anger had cooled. Mother took me in the end and said the others had colds. Aunt Lawrence commented with her worst half-smile: 'Well, Frances, we have seen so much of you lately we will be growing quite tired of your face. It is strange those two both getting colds at the same time, but they are so devoted. Curiously enough I saw them in the town this morning, about an hour ago, eating ice-cream from a barrow: not a very wholesome thing to do and, I may add, not very polite.'

Mother hung her head like a scolded child, but worse was to come. Uncle Lawrence turned to Mother, who was sitting on his left. He always slightly bowed his head when he started a conversation. 'Dora dear, I would appreciate it if your children did not pester me to lend them my valuable horses. If we had an old pony, or even a donkey, it would be another matter, but I can't have those children riding my hunters.' Ruby laid down her knife and fork and chimed in with: 'They are quite capable of breaking one of the horse's legs, and the poor thing would have to be shot.' To my surprise Grace scowled at her and said: 'Shut up, you fool. John is a marvellous rider, and I wish he could come riding with me sometimes. Couldn't he, Father?'

Uncle Lawrence ignored her and turned to a delicate-looking little woman on his right and started an amusing discussion about whistling horses as far as I could make out. In spite of her frailty, the visitor was a fearless huntswoman and much respected by the Lawrences.

Mother sat across the table, trying to manage her roast beef with shaking hands, while slow tears rolled down her soft, pink cheeks. Her uncle looked at her distastefully, sighed, then said: 'I might give the boy a bit of shooting later on. You can tell him that, Dora. I seem to remember he's quite a good shot for his age.' Mother said gratefully: 'Yes, indeed, he is an excellent shot. Thank you, Uncle.'

We had coffee in the drawing-room and Uncle Lawrence and the hard-riding woman drank brandy. One of her little kid gloves lay on the sofa beside me and I couldn't resist putting my rather stumpy little hand into it. It looked a lovely little hand in the elegant grey glove. I held it up in admiration and, forgetting where I was, cried: 'Oh! when I'm grown up I'll always wear gloves like this. I'll be a beautiful young widow of eighteen and live in Paris and I'll lift up my beautifully gloved, slender hand and say . . .' But I couldn't think what I'd say. 'I'll say: "Tickets, please." ' There was a horrible silence for a moment, then Aunt Lawrence reproved me: 'How can you be so vain, child? Take that glove off immediately, you'll split it with your podgy hands.' I hurriedly peeled the glove off, but the owner was charming about it, so my aunt couldn't be too hard on me.

When we got home we found John and Esmé playing chess in the garden, at least John was teaching Esmé to play chess. When Mother told John Uncle Lawrence's message about the shooting, the chess lesson was forgotten and he rushed upstairs to inspect his guns. He decided they needed cleaning and brought them down to the kitchen, and the scrubbed table was soon littered with guns and oily rags. We all sat around watching, except for the diligent Polly, who was using the sewing machine in the dining-room. Toby produced his pop-gun and that had to be cleaned too.

Four

ALTHOUGH THEY KNEW of my visits to Vanda, none of the family had met her or expressed any wish to. I preferred it like this, because I wanted to keep her to myself. If Vanda had become a family friend, it would not have been the same; also I knew that Polly wouldn't approve of her, and this might result in my not being allowed to visit the farm. I took the baby Jane home one afternoon, rather self-consciously pushing her rickety pram with its squeaking wheels. I had brushed her remarkably long, thin hair and, I thought, cleaned her quite successfully, but Mother thought otherwise and couldn't bring herself to touch her. 'Why, poor little mite, her ears are filthy and her head is all scurfy. No, I don't think I want to hold her, thank you, dear, she seems quite happy with you.' Then later: 'That child has a very sad expression on its face, like a little, ill-treated animal. I'd rather not see her again.'

I carried the baby into the garden to show to the rest of the family, but they were quite indifferent to her, except Clare, who produced her mouth-organ from a pocket in her knickers and played to her. This was most successful. We sat under our only tree, Jane clinging to me in her monkey-like way, laughing every now and then as she listened to the wavering music. A gentle wind rustled in the leaves and we were dappled with patches of moving sun. The hurt that Mother's reception of Jane had given me disappeared. I decided that she was never to see the inside of Vanda's house and I would do all I could to prevent them meeting. I knew that Vanda was insincere and selfish, but she was so pretty I couldn't help admiring and liking her. Maybe anyone would manage badly if they had been widowed so young and had so little money to live on. Ruby was almost in love with her, always bringing her name into the conversation, thinking of excuses to visit her, using her expressions and, what was more pitiful, trying to look like her.

Esmé accompanied me when I returned Jane to her mother. I tried to prevent her, but she continued walking beside me, and in a way I was glad, because I was embarrassed pushing the wretched little pram through the village. John had oiled the wheels, so the squeaks had diminished, but all the same it was an awful object to be seen pushing. Jane kept lolling about in a drunken manner, throwing her grimy pillow into the road every few minutes and sucking the straps of her pram. When we arrived at the farm the Major's motor-car was outside and there they were, sitting on the grass in front of the house, having drinks and looking very happy. Vanda's face lost its happy look when she saw that I had returned Jane earlier than she had expected. She asked if I would like to put Jane to bed. 'You know how you enjoy doing things for her, and you are so good at it.' I did not want Esmé to go into the house and I never liked being there when the Major was around, so I excused myself and left the pram in the middle of the lawn. I could see that Vanda was annoyed, and the baby was already crying because she did not want me to leave her.

As we walked away, Esmé said: 'I don't like the atmosphere of those people, and although I'm not particularly

54

interested in babies I'm sorry for that one.' We were both feeling slightly depressed as we turned towards the fields. Then I suddenly had the idea of showing Esmé my barn residence, which was quite near. I told her she was being taken to see something special that no one knew about, but, when we reached the barn, I could see that mud walls were just mud walls to her and the barn was a ruin. She tried to be nice about it and, when we climbed into the loft, she pretended to admire the window, which was a hole, and the chair-bookcase, which was a box, and the table-cupboard, which was also a box. I sat down on the box which was no longer a chair and thought rapidly while Esmé stood there looking bored. Then I asked in an off-hand manner: 'Have you ever seen a chair made of human skin?' She laughed and said she didn't think anyone had except in their imagination. Then I told her about the General's chairs. It took some time to convince her that they really existed, and then she became as determined to see them as I had been.

I soon wished I had never mentioned them, because she kept demanding to be taken to see them. Every morning before we went downstairs she would say: 'What about those skinny chairs? Let's pay your old general a visit today.' I kept explaining how difficult it would be to ring the door bell and summon that burning red face and say to it: 'Please, we have come to see your skinny chairs' or something similar, but on the third morning Esmé said impatiently: 'I'm not afraid of that old general. If you won't come with me, I'll go by myself. He may even offer to lend me a horse.' I don't know why, but I didn't want her to go by herself. Although I was frightened of them, perhaps I felt the chairs belonged to me, or it may have been that I wanted to be there to see her reaction to them. Anyway, I reluctantly agreed to go with her, adding: 'I think it will be better after tea, when it's growing a little dark. We may even be able to get into the house without him seeing us, and if that cheeky stable-boy comes out, you will be able to manage him.'

Later in the day I discovered it was Friday the thirteenth and told Esmé we had better delay the visit until the following day, but she wouldn't hear of it. As the day wore away I became more and more afraid and bitterly regretted ever mentioning the chairs. While we were having tea, John asked Esmé if she would like to practise golf with him. He had found Father's clubs in the cupboard under the stairs. Relief came over me in waves and I started to munch my bread and golden syrup happily. Esmé would never refuse to play golf with John. But I was wrong, for after a moment's consideration she replied: 'I might later, but I have promised to do something with Frances immediately after tea; I'll tell you about it later.'

Polly insisted that we both washed up the tea things before we left the house, so I had another reprieve, slowly drying cups and dropping as many spoons as I could and groping about for them under the sink; but I couldn't prolong the task for ever, and eventually we put our imitation leghorn hats on our heads and left the house.

When we were actually on our way, my terror of the General and Friday the thirteenth wore off a little and I hurried up the Straight Mile towards the village, almost trotting to keep up with Esmé, who had long thin legs and strode along.

When we reached the village, we saw Aunt Lawrence in her misty blue-grey tweeds crossing the green. She carried a walking-stick and her small black dog was prancing round her. With one accord we made a dive into Mrs Pugh's general shop and were engulfed in a smell of cats and very salt bacon. There was a large cat curled up on the top of almost every open sack and Mrs Pugh was often reluctant to disturb them when customers wanted to buy some of the contents. 'Wouldn't it be sugar you're needing, instead of rice?' she would ask plaintively. 'Or what about soda? The cats don't seem to fancy that.' Esmé had a few pennies with her, so we were able to buy some acid drops, which we loved, although they sometimes caused blisters on our tongue. When we left Mrs Pugh's shop, the village appeared to be clear of Lawrences – there was only their red house scowling at us through the iron railings – so we continued on our way, sucking and crunching sweets. We passed the nurse pushing the boy who had swallowed a brick in a push-chair, who recognized me and said in a bossy voice: 'You children had better hurry home, it is going to pour in a few minutes.' We looked up at the sky and saw heavy clouds had gathered. It seemed as if they were filled with black rain and I was afraid again. Esmé said it would be a good thing if it rained, because we could ask the General if we could shelter in his house, and he could hardly turn us away.

We hung about by the space where the gates were supposed to be, but no rain fell. Then we strolled a little way up the drive. The place appeared to be deserted. I wondered if perhaps the General's wife had persuaded him to leave the house, but among the weeds we noticed recent hoof-marks on the drive and, when we came nearer, we saw the door was open and knew that someone must be about. I said: 'Esmé, have you ever thought how terrible it would be if it rained black rain?' She didn't answer, and we reached the open door in silence and stood there for a moment, looking into the dark, flag-stoned hall. I whispered: 'Esmé, you'll do the talking, won't you?' She agreed, but I could tell by her voice she was growing nervous. I told her that the chairs were in the far part of the hall, so after some more whispering we decided to enter without ringing the bell, which would have been impossible anyway because someone had already pulled it right out and it didn't connect with anything. We cleared our mouths of acid drops and entered the hall. The grass had gone – someone must have poisoned it – and all that remained was shrivelled and brown. We crept down the dark part of the hall and came to the part where there was light showing through a window. There were the chairs just as I remembered them, heavy, dusty and sombre, looking as if they had been there for ever. Esmé touched the seat of one, slightly scratching it with her finger-nail, then quickly drew her hand away and whispered: 'Yes, they really are made of skin, and there is the light one you mentioned. How terrible! Oh, I wish we hadn't come.' When I had seen the chairs before, the sun had been shining and grown-up people had been chattering round them, but now all I could hear was an occasional heavy drop of rain on the window, and the very dust on the chairs was dismal – it seemed such dead dust, only disturbed in one place where Esmé's long hand had touched it. On the table there was a horrible biscuit-barrel with a ram's head for a lid. The horns were real horns, but the head was made of black metal. I knew that if there were any biscuits in the barrel, they would taste disgusting.

Esmé said: 'Let's go,' but as soon as she moved away, only one or two steps, there was a great thud as if someone had thrown down a huge sack of earth. It was followed by a rattling, snoring sound. I seized Esmé's skinny arm and we faced each other, too terrified to move. She said shakily: 'It's nothing, only someone snoring, but let's get out of here quickly.'

Carefully walking on our toes, we came to the main hall. It was very silent except for the sound of the rain, which was beating down now, and above the sound we could hear something that could have been heavy breathing. Esmé clutched me and hissed: 'Can you hear that? He's going to pounce.'

A door which had been closed before was now partly

open, and it was definitely from there that the breathing came. We stood still, not daring to pass it, then we moved forward very slowly and quietly and, although we were so afraid, we couldn't help looking through the open door as we passed. There was something very red and white inside – most likely a hassock, I thought, or even a huge cherry pie. Then we saw it was the General's head lying there by the door, and one eye was open and the other shut. The open eye saw us and he sort of gurgled and slightly moved one freckled old hand. We thought he was lying on the floor like that to frighten us; perhaps he was suddenly going to grab one of our legs.

'Do you think he is having a fit, or is it just a frightening game?' I asked Esmé, but she thought he was drunk and might at any moment attack us, so we left him there and ran out into the rain.

About half-way down the drive I stopped and told Esmé we ought to go back in case he had fallen and broken a leg. Now he couldn't pounce, I was feeling braver. Esmé told me to go back if I wanted to, and splashed on through the rain, and after standing for a moment irresolute I ran after her. We were wet through when we reached home and, as we changed our clothes in our bedroom, we both felt more and more depressed and afraid. It was as if we had great weights of sorrow on our chests and it was an effort to breathe. I kept saying: 'Suppose he really was ill and we left him there without even a cushion under his head?' and Esmé said: 'You have made me worried now, but I'm sure he was drunk, his face was so red.' She turned her back to me so that I could button up her dress and added: 'Once I saw a drunk tramp asleep under a hedge and he looked just the same.' I said despondently as we went downstairs: 'The General always had a red face.'

It never entered our heads to tell Mother or even Polly or

59

John. Our main concern was that no one should ever discover we had been near the General. In any case it seemed
dishonourable to enter a house uninvited and then tell people
we had seen the owner so drunk he was grovelling on the
floor. After our cold supper of salad and cheese we played
whist, even Polly joining in, and Mother played the piano.
It was only the old one that used to be in our school-room,
but it was the first time she had touched it since we moved
into The Hollies and it was reassuring to hear her playing
again in her strange way. She always kept a foot on one of
the pedals, loud or soft in turns, so it sounded like waves.
It was such a pleasant evening that our guilty depression
lifted and the General was forgotten.

The following morning was one of those brilliant mornings that seem too good to last, but are very enjoyable while
they do. We were all up early and by the time Mrs Hand's
hanging old face appeared round the door breakfast was
cleared away and we were awaiting for Polly to allot us our
various household tasks. Mrs Hand put down her black
American cloth bag and proceeded to hang her coat on the
kitchen door. 'Sad, isn't it?' she remarked with a sniff. 'Sad,
Mrs Hand?' Polly said in the rather bracing voice she used
when she spoke to servants. 'Sad? It's a lovely morning,
couldn't be better.' Mrs Hand looked reproachful. 'Yes, that
may well be, miss, but it's the old General I'm thinking of.
Dying all alone like that, on the floor too. It was little Jim,
the stable boy, that found him early this morning. Stark cold
by the door he was, so I should think he was trying to get
help. Poor old gentleman! Although he hadn't been here long,
it's quite upset me. If someone had been there to send for
the doctor, he'd most likely be alive today. It was a stroke,
they say. Poor old gentleman, he died worse than a dog.'

Five

ESMÉ SAID: 'The poor old chap was due to die, anyway.' Although she was shocked she did not feel guilty, but I did. I couldn't forget the movement of the freckled hand and that one mobile eye. I felt dreadfully guilty and unhappy inside, and if one feels like that, it's true. Perhaps the difference in our attitude to the General's death was due to the fact that I'd seen him alive, happily riding with the sun on his red face, and heard his gruff voice. Sleeping without sheets and having grass growing in his hall did not mean he was due to die, he just liked living that way. We didn't go to the funeral, but I believe a gun was shot over his grave and his coffin was carried to the church by soldiers. Mrs Hand and Ruby both told us about it in awed voices and even Aunt Lawrence said he was a dear old man and that, if his wife had looked after him properly, he would still have been alive. I liked to hear her say this, although I knew whose fault it was that he was not alive.

I was having nightmares again and on several occasions had disturbed the house with my screams. One night I awoke from a particularly bad dream and, as I lay shivering between the sheets, I saw through the parted curtains that the dawn was breaking. Then the idea came to me, vaguely at first, then more clearly, that if I visited the General's grave and spoke to him while no one was about, he might forgive me, even send a sign that he had done so. I managed to dress without disturbing Esmé, crept down the stairs and let myself out by the kitchen door. Except for the birds it was completely quiet in the garden as I stood there, watching the sky lighten in sudden waves. The leaves on our tree were still and slightly drooping, but, as the sun began to rise, the leaves rose too. It was as if they were waking up and breathing. I watched fascinated until it was completely light, then I hurried off towards the village.

Except for an old man carrying a sack on his back – and he did not want to be seen – I met no one, although people were awake. I saw smoke rising from a few chimneys and I heard someone chopping wood in a lonely way. A dog ran past me with a half-grown rabbit in its mouth and I found a hedgehog crossing the road at a leisurely walk. I carefully put it on a bank the way it was facing and hoped that was where it wanted to go. They were always getting squashed on the roads. There were some roses hanging over a green fence and I stopped and picked a few for the General's grave. They were whitish-green ones, with dew on the petals, and they smelt so lovely I held them up to my face so that I could smell them as I walked. When I reached the churchyard it was easy to find the grave I was looking for because it was roughly made of new earth, with faded pink-brown flowers piled upon it. I had expected a huge marble cross or something similar to be already there. Attached to the dead flowers there were visiting cards with messages written in smudged ink. It all looked very worn and untidy, not a suitable resting-place for a gruff general, hardly any better than the graves I'd made for the chickens who had died of the pip. I put the roses among the dry, dead flowers. I couldn't see any spare jam-pots or water about, so they would soon add

62

to the general untidy mess and it would have been better if I had left them growing. The grass was sparkling with heavy dew, too wet to sit on, so I stayed standing, looking down on the grave and trying to imagine the General lying there. I felt too shy to speak to the old man and I did not think he would hear me if I did. If his spirit was still earth-bound, it would most likely be in the stables with his horses. I tried saying the Lord's Prayer, but it didn't sound very good out in the open; perhaps it would have been better if I had knelt. I said: 'I'm sorry, General,' and felt better for saying it, but doubted if he heard. I stayed there, trying to think about being sorry, but my mind kept wandering and noticing things like the swallows' nests under the church roof and a robin that was watching me from a yew tree. How bright its rusty-red breast was against the dark green! I saw a stripy cat running through the long grass with a hunting expression on its face and I saw that it was stalking a damp Red Admiral drying its wings on a family tomb. It stopped and was wriggling its body like a golfer before he hits the ball, but just before it pounced I clapped my hands and it ran away. As I was leaving the churchyard, it came up to me in a friendly manner and rubbed itself against my black-stockinged legs.

I went home feeling much happier, although I did not feel I had made much contact with the General. During breakfast I asked Mother if the dead wreaths had been taken off Father's grave. She replied crossly: 'Of course, your father's grave is well tended. Davis visits it every week, and when the ground is settled a cross of Cornish granite will be placed there. Your Uncle Frederick has promised to pay for it and I only hope he keeps his word.' Mother sighed and the rest of the family gave me reproving glances over their porridge plates and I wished I hadn't spoken. John and Esmé were making plans to go shooting later in the day and Polly asked if they had

Uncle Lawrence's permission. John replied that they were only shooting rabbits and pigeons, and Uncle Lawrence had said something about him shooting, but of course he wouldn't aim at a pheasant unless he was with a proper shooting party. Mother agreed that something had been said about John being allowed to shoot, but she could not remember what.

After breakfast I made the beds with Mrs Hand. She was most particular about the clothes being tucked in at the bottom first, always remarking that, if you made the bed at the head, you would never be wed. It seemed more difficult making it that way, although I had to do it because I didn't want to be an old maid. This morning she told me that Vanda was without a nursemaid again. 'That poor little baby, I don't know what will become of it,' and she shook her flabby head. 'We don't want any more tragedies in the village. We haven't got over the old General's death yet.' I left her as soon as I could after that. I did not like it when people referred to the General in that way and hoped someone would come and live in his house as soon as possible so that people would forget about him. Of course I did not know then what a change in all our lives the next tenant would cause.

In the afternoon John and Esmé went off on their shooting expedition and from the dining-room I could hear Polly teaching the little ones their tables. I thought it a good idea to escape in case I was included in the lesson, and considered it a suitable time to visit Vanda and see how she was managing without a nursemaid's help. On the way there I met Ruby jerking along, her pale face poked forward. She seemed pleased to see me and we walked towards the farm together, Ruby chattering about her wrongs, how her mother called her a grampus, whatever that was, and how difficult she made it for her to visit Vanda. 'I have to creep out like a thief in the night, only it's afternoon,' she said dejectedly. 'Grace has more freedom than I.'

When we reached the farm the Major's car was there and I cried: 'Oh Ruby, I don't think I will stay. I hate it when the Major's there.' She persuaded me to stay; but I wished she hadn't because there was a feeling of badness about. We rang the bell, then knocked at the door in case the bell wasn't working, in fact we must have made rather a din, but no one came.

'Do let's go, Ruby,' I pleaded, 'they must be out somewhere, because the door is locked, and it's usually left open.' But Ruby was wearing her obstinate expression and was determined to get in. 'Of course they're not out. The car's there for one thing and I can distinctly hear Jane crying. Let's go round to the back of the house in case they are sitting in the garden.'

We walked round to the garden, if you could call it a garden, and all we saw was Jane's pram vibrating with screams. 'There, I knew they would be around somewhere,' she exclaimed and hurried to the pram and lifted the soaking, sobbing child out of it. There was a large purple-brown bruise on her forehead. 'Poor little thing, I wonder how she got that,' Ruby said as she held the messy bundle in her arms. Already the baby had ceased to cry and was giving a lopsided smile. Her tiny white legs hung down below the crumpled frock and, looking at them in dismay, I said: 'Ruby, her legs – should they be thin like that? And her face is so small. I'm sure she has shrunk since I saw her last.' Ruby wasn't listening, she was hurrying towards the house calling Vanda, Jane's little head lolling over her shoulder. Miserably I followed her and was just in time to see Vanda open the door. She was wearing a man's dressing-gown and her hair was hanging over her face. She almost snarled: 'What the hell are you making such a noise about? Am I never to be left

65

in peace?' Poor Ruby almost dropped the baby. She was speechless. I said shortly: 'It's Jane, she's bruised or something and she's sopping wet.' I hated Vanda as she put her hand to her head and peered at us through her hair in a dazed manner. Then she slowly said: 'Sorry, Ruby. I've such a splitting head I've been lying down.' Ruby spluttered: 'But where's the Major? I mean, his car is outside.'

Vanda said in a bewildered way: 'The Major? Oh Dick, yes, he was here earlier on, only I sent him away because of my head. He's down the fields shooting or something, but I expect he'll be back for his car later. Look, Ruby, could you be a lamb and mind Jane for a bit while I go back to bed? I feel awful – you know how it is at times. Take her for a walk, she'd love that.'

'Well,' Ruby answered doubtfully, 'I suppose I could, but I'll have to take her upstairs to change her nappy. She's in a frightful state.' Ruby had already managed to get into the hall and now she pushed past Vanda crossly and was heading for the stairs. Vanda turned and ran in front of her. 'No, no. Please don't go upstairs, the mess – it's quite unnecessary because there are some napkins on the line. I'll just go back to bed for half an hour and I'll be better when you return.' She was already half-way up the stairs and clutching both sides of the banisters. 'We'll all have tea together, shall we? Could you put a kettle on the oil stove, Frances? Good-bye, see you both in half an hour, but don't hurry.' She stood draped across the stairs until we trailed away to the kitchen. Even then, when she went into her bedroom she locked the door. I could hear the key grate in the lock. Ruby was already taking a napkin from the clothes-line and I was glad she did not hear it. It made one feel so unwelcome.

We trundled the pram down the lane. Jane was happily waving a blade of corn over her head, but Ruby looked shaken and her thin mouth dropped. After a bit she said:

66

'This seems to be my unlucky day: first Mother, now Vanda. It gave me such a shock when she spoke like that.' Her eyes filled with tears, which made them appear dimmer than ever. I tried to cheer her up by saying: 'It's most likely the Major's fault and they have had another quarrel. Don't worry, she'll be quite different when we go back.' And I was right. When we returned nearly an hour later, there was Vanda waiting for us in the lane, wearing a slimly cut, green linen dress which made her look like a daffodil leaf, her pretty face soft with fine powder. She said brightly: 'Dick came back, so I've sent him into the village to get some sticky buns or something sugary. My head's much better now. I think it was just a touch of the sun combined with drinking too much wine at luncheon. Dick brought a bottle with him and it was such a treat. I adore wine, don't you?' Ruby was still downcast and answered that she did not adore any drink. Vanda gave her a sharp look, then smiled and touched her shoulder lightly. 'I'm sure you are right, but don't be such an old sobersides. You see I want to ask you a favour and I can't while you are cross with me.'

Of course the favour was the usual one, minding Jane the following day while she went out with the Major. Ruby muttered: 'How can I look after Jane in the middle of the day? Mother would miss me at luncheon, and she wouldn't allow me to eat it here. She makes enough fuss about me coming as it is.'

After a lot of discussion it was arranged that I would give the baby her midday meal and Ruby would take over as soon as she could escape from home. It surprised me that I was allowed more freedom than Ruby, who was grown up and wore her hair in a sad little bun.

We had tea in the garden and the awful Major made his usual facetious remarks to Ruby, but at least they made her happy and soon she was squirming and giggling and giving him arch glances over her thick white teacup. He told her he would teach her to drive his car if she would give him dancing lessons – he was sure she knew all the latest steps. He also asked her if she painted her lips and, if she did, was it kiss-proof? That went down horribly well. Poor old Ruby, it was so easy to make her happy, but she was happy so seldom. Before I left the farm I gave Jane a bowl of groats and milk and, although it was a little burnt and lumpy, she appeared to enjoy it. She was covered in it before I finished feeding her with a spoon, but at least some of it had gone where it was meant to go. I wished I could feed her up and make her look like other babies and planned to bring some nourishing food with me the next day.

It must have been about seven o'clock when I arrived home. The front door was open, which looked queer in such a prim-looking house. It was as if its mouth hung open. I could hear a lot of excited talk and the most unusual sound of Esmé crying. My first thought was that someone else had died, but when I entered the sitting-room everyone was there. Mother was crying as well as Esmé, and John was shouting. 'The old beast, the blasted old beast.' Polly was looking flushed and annoyed and the two little ones had taken refuge under the table. I sank into a chair and regretted eating the Major's awful buns. It was some time before I discovered the cause of this new trouble that had come to us, because John and Esmé kept interrupting each other; then I gathered that, while they were shooting in Uncle Lawrence's spinney, one of the farm hands they had never seen before came up to them and asked if they had Mr Lawrence's permission to shoot over his land. John said that of course he had; Mr Lawrence was his uncle anyway. After that they went on happily shooting and collected a bag of three rabbits, two pigeons and four crows. They had specially shot the crows for Mrs Hand, whose husband was partial to a crow pie, she often told us. Suddenly Uncle Lawrence appeared from between the beech trees, waving his walking-stick and shouting: 'Leave my wood instantly. You are no better than thieves or poachers.' He came up to them in a towering rage and denied telling Mother that John had permission to shoot over his land; he may have said that he might ask him to join in a shoot some time, but he was damned if he would now. In spite of being called a thief or poacher, John apologized, but when Uncle Lawrence ignored his apology and went on muttering about poachers, he suddenly lost his temper and called him a mean old devil. John said: 'You know it was out before I could stop it.' Esmé said excitedly: 'Yes, and I called him a bloody liar.'

Polly asked in a low voice: 'What happened after that?' Esmé and John exchanged glances, then Esmé continued: 'Well, he went quiet after that, just said it was a pity to add blasphemy to our other crimes, and turned his back on us and started walking away. And then I did something I expect you will think terrible, but I'm glad I did it. I ran after him with all the things we'd shot, and I hit him in the face with a stiff, dead rabbit and flung the other bodies – the rooks and things – at his feet, and I'm glad I did, although I ran like mad afterwards.'

John said: 'Yes, I longed to follow her, but thought I'd better walk away in a dignified manner. But I felt pretty scared until I got off his beastly land. I expected he would set bloodhounds or the police on me at any moment. You know it was he who started the swearing, anyway.'

Poor Mother stood there looking bewildered, holding a chamois leather in one hand and a silver mirror she had been polishing in the other. That anyone should call her children thieves and poachers was outrageous, but they had sworn and insulted their elderly uncle and benefactor and Esmé had flung dead vermin in his face. He was the only man she had to turn to and now perhaps he would send them away from the village or make it too uncomfortable for them to continue living there. She was terrified that he would come to the house to complain and demand apologies, perhaps bringing Aunt Lawrence with him. All this came out in broken sentences and she ended by turning to Polly and imploring: 'What are we to do, Polly? Tell me what we are to do.' She so longed for her uncle's affection and good opinion, and now she felt she had lost it for ever.

Polly said thoughtfully: 'I think half the trouble is that Esmé and John haven't once bothered to go to Tower Hill Sunday luncheons. They went round there trying to borrow horses and, when that failed, they ignored the Lawrences, and they are not the sort of people who like being ignored. I can't imagine Uncle ever forgiving the swearing or rabbit-throwing.'

'Don't you think he would if they apologized?' Mother asked, slightly more hopefully.

Esmé blazed: 'We would rather die than apologize – that is, unless he apologizes to us first.'

Polly said slowly, as if she were doing a lot of considering in her mind: 'I agree, it would be rather difficult for them to apologize after being called thieves and poachers. I think the only thing to do is for us to go round to Tower Hill this evening, you and I, Mother. We might even find Uncle alone in his study.'

'What! Go and see him now?' Mother asked in a faltering voice. 'Wouldn't it be better if you went first? If he isn't very angry, you could ask him to come and see me in the morning. You are so good at managing people, Polly.'

Polly stood up and said firmly: 'No Mother, you will have to come too.'

'Oh dear,' said Mother, and then, brightening: 'We can't go now. They will just be sitting down to dinner.'

70

'We will go after dinner,' Polly said, relentlessly, as she tucked her blouse primly into her skirt as if preparing for battle.

'After dinner might not be so bad, perhaps. Men are supposed to be milder after a meal, aren't they? It's going to be a terrible ordeal all the same.' And Mother started to cry again.

John went to her, put his arm round her and said how sorry he was to have caused her so much trouble; it would be a good thing when he returned to school, there were only two more weeks of the holidays left in any case. This remark started us all off sniffing again, Mother saying through her tears that if only Father were alive these things wouldn't happen, and Esmé that she wished she was dead. Then Toby crawled from under the table and, showing a great hole in the heel of his sock, said sadly: 'If only Father were alive I wouldn't have socks like this.' It was a dreary evening, but eventually Polly organized us into drinking cocoa and eating bread and mousetrap cheese and then went off to the Lawrences, accompanied by a reluctant Mother.

When we had put the little ones to bed, John, Esmé and I sat humped up on the kitchen table, thinking our own thoughts. It was nearly eleven when they returned. Mother went straight upstairs without saying anything. Polly said it went off better than she had expected and ordered us all to bed.

The extraordinary thing was that the next morning one of the farm hands arrived with a large, newly killed cock, saying that it was for Mother with the master's compliments. The only birds that had come our way before were pigeons, so this must have been a 'heaping of coals of fire on our heads' sort of bird. It was only fit for boiling, though.

Six

BEFORE THE HOLIDAYS ENDED, Uncle Lawrence for-
gave John. He rode round to the house one morning and
asked him if he would like to have a day's shooting. John
would have preferred to refuse, but when he saw the expression on Mother's face he accepted, and he was glad afterwards, because he had a most agreeable day and brought back
a brace of pheasants. I don't think Esmé was ever forgiven,
but the Lawrences never had liked her for some reason. On
his last Sunday, John reluctantly accompanied Mother and
Clare to the usual Sunday luncheon at Tower Hill and afterwards played croquet with Grace. He got on extremely well
with Grace, which always annoyed us – he even liked her.
To his surprise, Aunt Lawrence presented him with a sov-
ereign. Mother was more pleased than he was and kept
repeating on the way home: 'They are so good to us, I don't
know how we would manage without them,' which made
John squirm.

The thought of losing John for twelve weeks depressed us
all, but Esmé and I had the high school weighing on our minds
as well. I knew I was backward, and it was months since I
had done any lessons. Esmé, who found learning easy, tried
to coach me a bit, but found it almost unbelievable that there

72

were such enormous gaps in my knowledge. She said it would take me at least a year to catch up with other girls of my age. The only French I knew was the verb 'to have' and the names of a few domestic animals and basic foods. My spelling was fantastic. History consisted of a number of amusing stories our governesses had read to us from a book called *Our Island Story* and the fact that Belgium was the 'cockpit of Europe', but no dates or hard facts. Geography was a list of names I had learnt by heart and maps. I was good at drawing maps, although I never connected them with real places; they represented just a flat peopleless world. My arithmetic had reached simple money sums. Someone had tried to teach me algebra but soon gave it up as hopeless. The only subjects I shone in were simple botany, drawing and composition. My ill-spelt compositions went on for pages and were always returned to me decorated with red ink corrections. Esmé said my drawing would be a help and might come in useful for botany illustrations, and that was the only hope she could give me.

We had to start at the high school on John's last day, when we had planned to spend the day having a paper chase, taking a picnic lunch with us. John walked the two miles to school with us and I hoped the girls would notice what a handsome brother we had. I had never seen the school, which was in a Victorian residential area of the town. I had imagined a huge square building behind great iron gates and was disappointed to see a domestic-looking red house, rather like Tower Hill except that it was decorated with turrets. The large green gates were kept open by a brick, and girls dressed in navy blue were pouring through, satchels on their backs, and some carrying hockey sticks. They looked like the girls in school stories until I got closer and saw that they were a bit untidy and had things like gold bands on their teeth, spectacles and crooked seams on their black-stockinged legs. I was wearing a gym dress that Esmé had outgrown and

73

feeling a little ashamed of turning up at a new school in my sister's old clothes. John carried a small case containing our sandwiches and pencil-boxes, and was embarrassed by the sight of so many girls. He pushed the case into Esmé's hand, hurriedly said good-bye and crossed the road.

That first day at school was not so bad as I expected. The worst part was when most of the girls trooped off into the dining-room and we had to eat our sandwiches in one of the classrooms. The only other occupant was a particularly plain girl wearing a patched plaid blouse and eating a pork pie. She said she adored eating pork pies and ate them in her bath. She told us she was always hungry, like a mole, which was liable to die if it wasn't fed every two hours. She also ate corned beef in bed. She inquired if we had brought sandwiches because we were poor. Her father was, because he wrote religious books that did not sell well. Esmé said: 'We are dreadfully poor, almost starving in fact,' and I added that we had only recently become poor. Unlike Esmé I suffered from false pride.

In spite of being so backward I was put in a form consisting of girls more or less my own age, and my few accomplishments, and the fact that one of the girls was a mental defective, kept me from being quite at the bottom. If Esmé had not helped me, I don't think I should have been able to manage my homework – she did most of it for me. She became immensely popular immediately, in spite of having a sandwich lunch, and as a younger sister I shared a little in her glory. The worst thing I can remember about those two terms I spent at the high school was the long walk there and back with the telegraph wires humming overhead, often in bitterly cold or wet weather, and the boredom. The games bored me even more than the lessons. That awful hockey in a slushy field! Even now, if I see a pair of goal-posts in a flat field it gives me a feeling of doom. I remembered the

girls' red fat cheeks wobbling as they ran with elastic strain-
ing under their round chins – wretched hat elastic, always
too tight or too loose! The captain of the junior hockey team
used to pull mine tight and let it click back until it stung
me. She said it was to pay me out for having curly hair and
puffing as I ran.

School took up so much of my time that Vanda and her
baby almost passed from my mind. I had not heard anything
about them from Ruby either, because she was away from
home visiting relations in the north of England. They were
giving a coming-out ball for her, which we considered rather
silly, since she had already attended a hunt ball and had had
to spend most of the evening dancing with her brother. She
still kept the frosted dance-card with the little white pencil
hanging from it pinned over her bed beside the painting of
a woman sitting on top of the world twanging a broken harp.

Mrs Hand turned up one Saturday morning, wearing the
bloodhound face she put on when there was bad news. We
dreaded seeing it coming round the kitchen door. This morning she shuffled in with the face showing over her dirty fur
collar. 'I always knew it,' she croaked. 'Didn't I tell you? I
said there would be a tragedy over that child and now I'm
proved right. The poor little mite is in hospital and they don't
know if she will live. Pneumonia she's got, caused by neglect
as sure as I stand here.' Mother vaguely inquired: 'What
child are you talking about, Mrs Hand?' but I immediately
knew that it was Jane. Mrs Hand leant over the broom she
had taken from the cupboard and looked as if she had settled
there for the morning. 'Why, that widder woman's child, her
at the farm, the one Miss Frances is so keen on. She was
taken to the hospital yesterday with this pneumonia, double
I should say. It's a crying shame. You only had to look at
that child to see it was neglected.' 'Yes, poor child,' Mother
agreed. 'I remember noticing she had a dirty scalp. Why,

75

where are you going, Frances? Polly hasn't made out the shopping list yet.'

I was struggling into my coat and, as I left the house, shouted: 'I'm off to the hospital to see Jane if they will let me, and, if they won't, at least they will let me know how she is.' I had remembered noticing a building called The Cottage Hospital on the way to school and wondering why it was called 'cottage' when it did not in the least resemble one.

The hospital was nearly two miles away and I ran most of the way and arrived there breathless and untidy, which did not make a good impression when I rushed into the hall demanding to see Jane. A calming-down sort of woman pushed me down on a shiny bench and told me to wait. Sitting opposite to me were two people who appeared as if they were growing there: one an old man with a deep slimy cough, and the other a bearded woman. They did not appeal to me at all; I was particularly put off by the bearded woman, in case the beard was catching. When I was almost a baby I wouldn't let my nurse come near me because of the moustache above her lip, and eventually the poor thing had to be sent away. For years afterwards I used to petition God in my prayers not to let a moustache grow on my face.

I looked away from my companions and tried to concentrate on the brilliantly polished floor, finding indistinct pictures in the wood. Suddenly the main door was flung open and Vanda, wearing a little brown cap on the back of her head, burst into the hall and dramatically rushed up to the calming-down woman, crying: 'I must see my child. Let me see my baby.'

The woman asked her in a cold voice if she was Jane Martin's mother, then went off to fetch the sister in charge of the children's ward. When Vanda noticed me sitting on a bench like a patient, she asked what on earth I was doing there, then, bursting into tears, kept saying: 'My baby, my baby! It's not my fault she's so ill. Do you remember how careful I was and all the orange juice I gave her? I'd bought the material to make her a little dress, although I have never had time to make it. Now perhaps she will die and never wear it.' The sobbing increased at this point and the old people on the other bench began to take an interest. I remembered the material she referred to because it had been lying half-wrapped in paper on Vanda's chest of drawers for months and she had repeatedly asked Ruby if she would like to make it up, but Ruby did not sew. In spite of her crying, Vanda still looked very lovely and I began to feel really sorry for her.

The sister came sailing in, accompanied by a young doctor with a stethoscope hanging round his neck, and Vanda rose to meet them, holding a handkerchief to her glittering eyes and looking so young and fragile it seemed impossible that she was a mother. I couldn't hear much of what the sister was saying, but gathered that Jane was putting up a good fight in spite of the fact that she was suffering from malnutrition. Vanda became quite hysterical at the word 'malnutrition'. I did not know what it meant myself, but she apparently knew only too well.

'Malnutrition,' she almost screamed. 'Do you think I starved my baby? I was always giving her orange juice and little things to drink. Groats for instance. I bought tins and tins of groats. You can come and see the empty ones, if you like.' The young doctor touched her gently on the arm and said he was sure she had done her best, but in Jane's case it hadn't been quite good enough. Vanda said sadly: 'I did my best, but I'm only twenty-four. How should I know how to look after a baby? I'd hardly seen one before she was born and I've had to bring her up all alone.' I saw she had made a good impression on the doctor, but the nurse kept her lips firmly pressed together and flicked her stiff cuffs. Eventually she opened her thin lips to ask if I was a patient. I told her the reason I was waiting and, while Vanda and the doctor talked together in low voices, she told me about Jane. She lost her hard expression and was really nice to me, treating me almost as if I was grown up. She said that, if Jane managed to live through the next two days, she would most likely recover, and she considered she had a good chance in spite of the condition she was in. She told me I could telephone every day to inquire if I liked and that I'd be allowed to see Jane on my way back from school one afternoon soon. I felt quite reassured after listening to the sister and went away without seeing any more of Vanda, who had gone up to the children's ward, accompanied by the doctor.

Four days later I was allowed to see Jane. The sister explained to me that children were not allowed to visit the hospital in the ordinary way, but Jane was an exceptional case and they thought I might be good for her. She took me upstairs and into a long ward containing clean children of all ages, and there was Jane behind the cretonne screen. When she saw me she smiled and lifted up her arms, as if wanting me to take her from the cot. She looked a strange colour, blue in places, and her lips were dry and cracked, but she was wonderfully clean, and her long hair was tied up in a queer little knot on the top of her head. Seeing her there giving me such a welcome made me realize how fond of her I was. With her thin little face and bright eyes she looked so like a bird, the sort that fall out of their nests far too young. I sat beside her cot and put one of my hands through the bars, and she held it tight with both of hers until she fell asleep. The sister, who became a friend of mine, allowed me to visit her most afternoons for the entire month she remained in hospital. Vanda was away for part of the time, so they came to depend on me as a visitor; it was as if I was her elder sister. While Jane was in hospital, she learnt how to pull herself up, and towards the end of her stay was walking round the cot, holding on to the bars.

At home things went on pretty much the same, with Mother floating vaguely around and Polly managing everything. Poor girl, she worked so hard, but none of us was grateful, unless it was Mother. We had almost grown to dislike her, and when we heard her sharp tread on the tiled hall floor we would say: 'Quick! Polly's coming,' and hide whatever we were doing like conspirators. I think she must have felt very alone, and perhaps that accounted for the Golden Boy episode.

The Golden Boy was a last-year student at the grammar school, but, unlike the other grammar school boys, he had a certain glamour, and we had once overheard him tell a man in a petrol station – he was always hanging around garages – that he was joining his parents in the Middle East when he had finished his education. Although he was a boarder, he used to stroll around the town capless, his golden hair flowing and glowing in the sun, which always seemed to be shining on him. He walked with a casual grace and often had a faint smile on his face, which I thought attractive but Esmé said was a smirk. It was I who christened him the Golden Boy, and Esmé who remarked that all that glitters is not gold. Eventually we just called him Goldy and, although Polly didn't join in our discussions about him, somehow she managed to make his acquaintance during one of her many shopping expeditions in the town. It was Clare who first whispered to me that Polly talked to Goldy in the street and that once he had carried her shopping basket all the way home. Then he started haunting our road (which was the sort of road that people didn't walk down for pleasure) in a purposeful manner, sometimes slightly smiling, sometimes slightly whistling and sometimes bending down to tie his shoelaces, which always seemed to come undone outside our house. Gradually we realized that there was something about The Hollies that attracted him to our depressing road. Even Mother observed him: 'That good-looking boy always seems to be passing the window. He looks too nice to live in one of those dreadful houses, but I expect people say the same about us.'

It was about this time that Polly started taking lonely walks on Sunday afternoons while we, if we were not otherwise occupied, would all curl up round the fire and make it roar up the chimney. Miniature red fires would start on the sooty back of the fire and the little ones would draw a line through them with the poker and pretend they were invading armies – the side which burnt the longest won the battles. As the children played with the fire or rolled plasticine on the carpet, making snakes or pressing it on newspaper so that the print came off on its dirty surface clear enough to read, Esmé and I pored over the novels borrowed from school friends. Any proposal of marriage we read aloud to each other with great feeling, but the bits we enjoyed most of all were the ones where the heroine refused her suitor with 'I love another'. As we amused ourselves in our various ways, Mother would doze in her chair, sometimes opening her eyes and saying in bewildered surprise: 'I almost went to sleep. It is cosy this afternoon; I can't think why.'

The Christmas holidays came, but there were no berries on our holly bush, just dust. I always suspected it was that kind of holly. John came home, bringing a goldfish aquarium he had made at school. It looked most professional until it was filled with water, which it was incapable of containing. John kept saying: 'Just wait until the putty dries,' but it didn't make any difference and eventually I turned it into a miniature greenhouse. We were so happy to have him home again and there were no upsets with the Lawrences this time, who even allowed him to ride with Grace once or twice. No mount was provided for Esmé, though. Mother was rather tearful on Christmas day, the first after Father's death, but it was not so bad as it might have been, despite everyone staring at us when we trooped into the church. It was the first time we had been since we came to the village and Polly insisted it was the thing to do, although Mother begged to be allowed to stay at home and roast her goose. Aunt Lawrence had given us the goose and came round later in the day to smell it cooking. We were each presented with a pair of grey woollen gloves, even Clare, who only had one hand. I knew these gloves well, because one of Old Nanny's tasks was to knit them for the poor of the village. The Lawrences smelt their goose, the whole house smelt of it. Aunt Lawrence said how fortunate we were to have such a comfortable home and we must all help our little mother as much as possible. She pulled Clare's lower eyelids down so that they looked ugly and said she was anaemic, and that I should have my hair cut short because it was too long and curly to be healthy, and that Polly should wear a snood. Then she kissed us all with her soft lips that smelt of sherry, collecting her walking-stick and husband, and walked away into the rat-coloured December dusk.

Goldy usually stayed at school during the holidays and John soon noticed him hanging round the house and started teasing Esmé, saying he was her 'follower'. This made her furious and she would shout: 'Can't you see he has a self-satisfied smirk? I hate the boy. It's Frances he comes to see. She's always talking about him and calls him the Golden Boy.'

John started to tease me about him then and said he must be a train-spotter because his shoes were so clean – train-spotters always cleaned their shoes at Malvern. John's teasing made me feel ashamed of my secret admiration for Goldy and I was relieved when Polly put a stop to it by saying:

'You're being awfully boring, John. That boy has a perfect right to walk past our house. I happen to know that he has relations living in the next road.' She went on about his good manners and how he sometimes carried heavy shopping-baskets for her. Then we forgot about him because he did not pass our house any more.

During the holidays I went to see Vanda once or twice. Jane was with her mother again. She had completely recovered and was looking just like other babies, with pink cheeks and a row of little white teeth in her mouth. The nurse had taught her to say a few rather silly words like 'ta' for 'thank you'; otherwise I felt very happy about her. A motherly sort of woman came to help Vanda every day and the house seemed more comfortable with her in it and the kitchen wasn't in such a mess. Jane was clean too, not quite as clean as she was in the hospital, but about as clean as the average village boy. Once I pushed the pram into the village and was surrounded by inquisitive women all wanting to see the baby that had almost died of double pneumonia.

Seven

MRS HAND told us that a middle-aged 'gent' had bought
Springfield, the General's old house, and it was to be repaired
and decorated. In fact, her husband had been engaged to do
some of the painting. Then Aunt Lawrence told us the man
was not a 'gent' at all, but a retired brass-founder. He was
rolling in money, he owned an appalling Birmingham accent
and would be quite impossible to know. I imagined him rolling in brassy coins all alone and felt sorry for him planning
to live in a village where no one would know him. It was
some weeks before I actually saw him because I did not pass
the General's house more often than I needed. An old parlour-
maid of the Lawrences, who had known Mother as a girl,
lived in one of the near-by cottages and I had to call there
to collect a young walnut tree she had promised Mother.
Although walnuts are about the slowest-growing tree you can
plant, Mother wanted one to remind her of the walnut trees
we had growing in the garden at home. 'A little one will be
better than nothing and we can move it when we leave,' she
said hopefully. She always imagined we would return to our
old house in the near future, although no one else did.

I had left the old parlour-maid's musty-smelling cottage
(she was called Mrs Millership, which seemed to add to the

smell). She had said good-bye to me about seven times on her doorstep and was still waving to me when I reached Springfield's mud wall. I was walking along with this lumpy newspaper parcel with earth dropping from it all the time, feeling sorry for poor lonely old Mrs Millership, when I suddenly came on the brass-founder looking exactly as a brass-founder should look, at least the body part of him. He was tall and burly, and what made him appear even larger than he was was his enormous brown overcoat, which almost reached the ground. He had smooth black hair parted on one side and later I noticed he had a double crown. His moustache was thin and drooping, a little like the ones men wear in the illustrations to *The Arabian Nights*. His head appeared small and bird-like compared with his large body. It would have easily fitted a smaller man. He was standing by a monster of a motor-car, the most exciting one I had ever seen, and I discovered later it was Spanish – a Hispano-Suiza – which had been made specially for him. He was standing there in the middle of the road writing something in a notebook. He must have heard the sound of clods of earth falling as I passed, because he turned from his notebook, gave me a penetrating glance and said: 'Wait a minute, child, and I'll wrap that thing properly for you.' Surprised and shy, I thanked him and stood still while he finished his notes. Then he produced some sacking from the back of the car, rummaged about until he found a piece of string and quickly and neatly packed the tree so that it appeared as if it had come from a nursery. He was so quick about it that we hardly spoke and he drove away before I could thank him properly. There was just a roar and a flash of moving red metal and he was gone and I was alone in the road with my little tree which smelt bitter and walnutty, although it had no leaves.

As I walked home I thought: 'Even if he isn't a gentleman, he's a magnificent sort of man.' I tried to remember his name, but I had never heard it mentioned because he was usually referred to as 'a middle-aged gent' or 'that brass-founder' in my hearing.

The following morning Mrs Hand came out with the information that my new friend was called Blackwell and that he had been a widower for some years. She added that it would take weeks before the General's house would be ready for him to live in because he was having so much done to it. There were to be extra bathrooms and wallpaper as thick as velvet and paintwork all to be a glittering white. She told us: 'It does seem a waste on a lone man, but it's bringing money to the village, so we can't complain.' She said this brightly as she tucked in the bottom sheet of Mother's bed. Her husband had been out of work most of the winter, hence the bloodhound's face. He was not a local man, so, if anyone had to be out of work, it always seemed to be him.

It was Saturday – a holiday – and one of those days when you can feel spring before it has started, a soft sort of day when you see white violets flowering in the banks if you look carefully. After luncheon Polly disappeared and we were free to do as we liked. Esmé went off to have tea with a school friend and Clare and Toby were digging up apples they had buried in the garden some time ago; for some reason they always imagined they would turn to coal if they were left in the ground long enough. Mother was in another corner of the garden in raptures because a rose tree she had planted in the autumn was actually sprouting tiny shoots. 'I think I shall take up gardening seriously, dear,' she said happily. 'Perhaps your uncle would let me have some plants, and a few tools wouldn't cost much. I have a trowel already and the coal-shovel does very well as a spade.' She looked so young working in her funny pointed garden, not at all like a poor widowed mother of six children. Everyone seemed to have something to do except me, so I decided it was time I had a look at my mud barn. I had not visited it all the winter, in fact I'd hardly thought of it for months, but now I was in a panic in case it had fallen down. I went through the fields, stopping every now and then to search for four-leaved clovers without success, then suddenly came on the barn in its kindly solitude, red-brown in the afternoon sun with the black old doors still open. I went in and stood near the door, looking about. It was just as it used to be – the pile of sacks, the bits of rusty iron and the remains of a huge carriage umbrella. But it didn't feel the same. For one thing there was an empty cigarette-packet lying on the floor, a fresh green one, and there was a sort of rustling going on above as if rats were playing. I kicked the doors and the rustling ceased, but I heard something like a stifled laugh and whispering and knew people were in my loft, perhaps even drinking out of my little cups and reading my books, and I felt afraid as if there was something evil about. Then someone cried: 'No, no!' and there was more laughter. I ran from the shed and, on an impulse, shut the double doors, securely fastening them by slipping a small iron bar through the hasp.

'They can stay there and starve for all I care,' I muttered and walked away. It wasn't only people being in my loft that upset me, it was the secret fear of what they were doing.

When I returned home, there was Mother sitting by a newly-lit fire wearing a pink tea-gown trimmed with fluffy brown feathers. She said: 'I'm tired of wearing dark colours. I've been going through all my clothes and intend to wear them, even if they are not quite suitable. After all, it's an economy.' She sat there looking just as she used to when Father was alive. We had iced chocolate cake for tea too. It had been intended for Sunday, but Mother said she could easi.y make another. Polly was not there to say it was an extravagance. She had gone to the Lawrences to fetch a recipe for making lemon curd and did not return until it was

86

dark because she had lost her watch when she was crossing the village green and it had taken hours to find it. She absent-mindedly cut herself a slice of chocolate cake, but after one bite put it down and said reproachfully: 'You shouldn't have started the cake. You are all so greedy as soon as my back is turned.' She piled the dirty tea-things on a tray and left the room, but I noticed she finished the piece of cake. When she had gone we let Esmé's mice loose in the sitting-room, although they didn't seem to enjoy it much, keeping close to the skirting board most of the time. There used to be a girl in our village who was continually beaten by her parents and I remembered she used to walk like that, close against the walls.

For a few days it seemed as if spring had come, then it went right back to winter. As Esmé and I trudged to school, we would moan for our lost bicycles, which had vanished in the great sale. Our fingers were swollen with chilblains and the backs of our heels were sore and rough, although we wore woollen stockings. During the school lunch-break we would sit on the radiators, munching our thick, dry sandwiches. The girl who ate pork pies said we would get piles, but we thought it worth the risk. The thing I was really afraid of getting was leprosy. I read about lepers in the Bible and *Ben Hur* first, then I found them appearing in other books and a missionary came to the school and told us about them and how they rotted away alive and had to go about ringing a little bell. Sometimes during the night I thought I could hear their bells ringing and would get up to close the window in case they climbed in. I drew pictures of how they looked and then became terrified of my own pictures. I felt better while I was drawing them, but it was afterwards I was so afraid. Esmé never felt afraid of things as I did and I kept my secret fears from her as much as I could.

When the weather was good, we used to sing together as

87

we walked to school, or run from one telegraph post to another with the wires humming over our heads. Sometimes we had time to look in the shop windows on the outskirts of the town. There was a tailor's shop with a model of a dappled horse in the window and a fascinating girl wearing a riding habit sitting side-saddle on it – always the same dark grey habit with the skirt in graceful folds. Occasionally the old tailor himself would be supervising the opening of his shop and gradually we became friendly with him. He often said: 'Young ladies, if you want to develop a beautiful throat and bust, throw your head back and gargle every morning.' He was also a great admirer of Ruskin and was always recommending us to read his books. Once he mentioned that Ruskin's marriage had been annulled and, when his papery cheeks crimsoned, we knew there was something embarrassing and interesting about this. We tried to find out from our English mistress, but never succeeded. There was also a second-hand bookstall we sometimes patronized. I bought several natural history books there, which had old-fashioned, detailed illustrations and were usually written by Reverends. Once we bought half a leather-covered book. We thought it might be valuable because it was so old and we liked the title, *The Way of Love*. When we read it, we found it was a queer, upsetting sort of book about things like women dressing up as nuns to attract men, or how, if a woman showed a little petticoat below her skirt, men would follow her for miles. Eventually we became disgusted and sickened and buried the book in the garden. The children dug it up later and it had become beautiful, all spotted with pink and green.

Now the Golden Boy did not pass our house any more we forgot about him until Aunt Lawrence came with her revelation. We had been feeling rather kindly towards her, because she had presented Esmé and me with a huge slab of delicious hunting cake to take to school with us. It was wonderfully sustaining and lasted us for days. Esmé pointed out that the Lawrence family wouldn't be needing hunting cake while the frost continued and there was no hunting, but agreed that it was kind of her to give it to us instead of storing it away in tins. And now in the dusk Aunt Lawrence came to say fearful things. Esmé and I were doing our homework in the dining-room when she arrived. We saw her passing the holly bush and noticed that the handsome face beneath the grey felt hat was flushed and that her lips were set in a straight line. No half-smile. Esmé said: 'Trouble's brewing,' and nervously wiped her pen on her bloomers. Although I couldn't bring any particular crime to mind, I felt guilty as I heard her open the front door and call: 'Is anyone at home?' in a haughty voice, and then: 'Where are you all?' Fortunately she had not seen us through the window and we crouched over our books, hoping she would not attack us first, but we knew that Polly was washing the little ones' hair in the kitchen sink and was unlikely to answer the summons. To our relief Mother came hurrying downstairs and we heard her kiss Aunt and take her into the drawing-room and it was quiet for a minute or two, just their low voices mingling. We were wondering if it was safe to draw the curtains and turn up the lamp when we heard a protesting cry from Mother: 'No, no, it isn't true. It must be a mistake. Ruby mistook her for someone else.' Then natter-natter and a loud 'You shouldn't come here to tell me such stories about my girl.' The drawing-room burst open and Mother's voice wailed: 'Polly, Polly! Come here at once.'

Polly, busy with the children, took a little time to answer and Mother had to fetch her. Esmé was called to finish the head-washing and I crept into the kitchen behind her, smelling the sweet and comforting smell of baked potatoes combined with shampoo.

As we dried the children's hair on the towels Polly had

thoughtfully put to air by the range, we whispered together. Which girl had Aunt come to complain about? Surely not Polly?

'Do you think it is because I go with Ruby to see Vanda?' I asked. 'Or that awful book we bought? She couldn't know about that.'

Esmé shook her head thoughtfully and said: 'I think it is something to do with Polly. She's been different lately, quieter and kinder. Perhaps she has a lover. Haven't you noticed she's always going for solitary walks and mooning about?' I whispered in horror: 'You don't think she's been meeting a man?' The sort of man I imagined was sinister and middle-aged with a black moustache with waxed ends and a diamond ring, most likely Italian. 'No, Polly would never meet a man,' I said reassuringly.

The drawing-room door cracked open and we heard Polly scream: 'You evil-minded old woman, trying to make trouble!' and before we could reach the hall she had gone away into the darkness outside. The front door was slightly swinging in the icy wind and, although Esmé ran to the front gate calling, there was no answer. We didn't expect one really. Mother came out of the drawing-room, shaking; her face was wet with tears. It was an inside sort of shaking; Esmé and I had it too. The children had followed us into the hall and were standing in their night things, their hair all wet and their feet bare. Aunt Lawrence said quite kindly: 'Frances, take those children back into the warmth. They will catch their deaths in this draught.' Toby kept asking: 'What's she done to Polly? She was going to give us baked potatoes with butter inside and read to us because we didn't cry when she washed our hair.' I took them back into the kitchen and tried to comfort them and hear what was going on in the hall at the same time. I heard Aunt Lawrence say that Mother was not to worry too much, but should be stricter with her daughters in future. 'I never trusted the girl myself, far too headstrong. It might be wise to have the girl examined by a doctor, but we don't want any scandal, of course. Things may not be as bad as they could be, perhaps the girl isn't ruined.' After that came Mother's 'How can you speak like that about Polly? She's only a child.' Then more nattering until Aunt said she was sorry to leave Mother, but she would be late for dinner as it was. 'I'll be over first thing in the morning,' she added as she left, and I sighed because I knew she would keep her word.

When we had put the little ones to bed, Mother, between fits of weeping, tried to tell us Polly's crime. It seemed she had been meeting Goldy secretly and they had been seen by one of the Tower Hill servants sitting on a haystack together, smoking. Ruby had picked up this piece of servants' gossip and had followed Polly the previous afternoon and seen her meet Goldy on the towpath. They had walked with their arms round each other. Mother had a fresh burst of tears at this point, then continued: 'She said, when she told her mother: "Really, Mother, I couldn't believe it was my own cousin walking in that disgusting way. She looked so common, like a village girl, and her petticoat was showing at the back." ' Esmé and I exchanged startled glances, but Mother didn't notice and went on incoherently: 'Oh dear, poor little Polly, she was the prettiest baby of you all, and now Aunt says she is ruined and no one will ever marry her. She said such hurtful things to the girl, no wonder she has run away. I'm sure there was nothing wrong between her and that stupid boy. Whatever has happened it must have been his fault,' Mother said firmly as she walked up and down the hall. 'The poor girl has had far too much responsibility for her age. Such a dreary life for a young girl! If only your father was alive, such terrible things would not occur. I don't know how to manage on my own, that's the whole trouble.'

91

Every now and then Mother would open the front door and peer out into the night, while cold air poured into the narrow hall, then she would wander round the house, ending up in the kitchen, where she would huddle up in the old wicker armchair and the tears would start again. 'Aunt shouldn't have spoken to her like that. Poor child, all that housework and no pleasures, no friends of her own age. I know I'm to blame. She wouldn't have taken up with that wretched boy if she'd been happier at home. It's all Ruby's fault. She's a real mischief-maker. Petticoat showing indeed!' Mother went on and on, blaming everyone except Polly. Her loyalty and faith touched me and I knew she would feel the same about any of us that were in real trouble.

When the hands on the kitchen alarm clock passed eleven, Mother became quite hysterical and said she was sure that Polly had drowned herself in the canal or been run over in the dark or murdered. As the miserable evening had progressed, an idea had been slowly forming in my mind and at last I said I thought I knew where Polly might be hiding.

'Why didn't you say so before?' Mother demanded crossly. 'If you know where she is, we had better go and bring her home.'

'It's only an idea,' I said nervously. 'I don't know for sure, but if I had a lantern I could go and look. It's over a mile away down the fields, and then she may not be there.'

We started searching for the lantern and discussing who was to accompany me on my search. It all became rather complicated. Mother said I was not to go alone, because she did not want to have two children murdered on the same night, but at the same time she would not come with me in case Polly returned and she were not there to welcome her. Then Esmé said she would join me, but that was not suitable, because Mother could not bear to be alone with her terrible thoughts 'and that beastly clock's hands moving all the time'.

After innumerable arguments and suggestions I was allowed to leave the house with my hurricane lamp and a box of England's Glory matches in my pocket in case it blew out. I did not tell Mother and Esmé exactly where I was going or my reason for going there, but felt certain I should find Polly hiding in my mud barn. I connected the cigarette-packet I had found on the barn floor with the fact that Polly had been seen smoking. Those whispering voices could have been Polly and Goldy's. I only hoped he wasn't with her now.

I walked in the night with my lantern, and disturbed owls cried as they hunted for field-mice. I did not mind them; it was the bats I was scared of as they swooped and flickered round me, squeaking in the dark. The earth was still hard with frost and sometimes long brambles entwined themselves in my skirt and I had to put the lantern down while I freed myself. Once I stumbled and the lamp went out and I couldn't manage the matches with my gloved hands. The complete darkness had made me afraid and I remembered the lepers and imagined they were peering through the hedges at me. When I at last got the lamp burning again, I warmed my hands against the glass and, to steady myself, read the joke on the back of the matchbox and tried to laugh. At last I reached the barn. The doors were closed and for a moment I thought the real owner must have padlocked them. I held the lantern high and saw what I had mistaken for a padlock was an old boot-polish tin someone had nailed on the door, perhaps to use for airgun practice, because it was riddled with holes.

I opened the door as gently as I could so as not to disturb Polly if she was sleeping in the loft. As I climbed the ladder, I heard the straw rustling and knew that it could be rats or even a tramp. I stood half-way up, too afraid to move. It was still again now. Whoever was there would see the light coming up through the hole in the floor. Somewhere near a

dog started frantically barking, and I thought the farmer
might have seen the moving light and be coming to investi-
gate. The rustling started again and I made myself climb
through the hole, putting the lantern through first. As I put
my head through I heard an ear-splitting scream – a girl's.
There in the straw was Polly with both her hands knuckled
round her mouth. She had straw in her hair, her drooping
eyes were inflamed and I could hardly recognize her. The
awful thing was that she reminded me of the mad Mrs
Rochester in *Jane Eyre* and I was almost as scared as she
appeared to be of me. After we had both stared at each other
for about a minute, I whispered: 'I've come to fetch you,
Polly. No one is angry with you at home, but Mother's dreadfully worried. She says it's all Ruby's fault, anyway.' She
asked in a strange, hoarse voice: 'How did you know I was
here? I suppose it was you that locked us in that time and
these are your books and things.' She looked round the dimly-
lit loft and shivered. 'You can't expect me to come home and
have Aunt Lawrence saying disgusting things to me as if I
was some kitchen maid that had got into trouble. It would
be better if I went away and never returned. If only people
hadn't interfered! There is such a little time left before Nigel
goes to Cyprus to join his parents. We would just have seen
each other three or four more times perhaps. But now the
Lawrences have spoilt everything. I never want to see him
again.' She was crying angry tears, not frightened ones, and
she was plucking the straw from her hair as if an enemy
had put it there. It was bitterly cold and I suddenly felt
overwhelmed with tiredness and wished I was older and knew
how to manage Polly. I said: 'Well, you'd better come home
now and discuss it with Mother, she's definitely on your side.
Don't let's stay here any longer. I believe there are a lot of
lepers in the hedges and I want to be at home.'

Polly gave me a haughty stare. 'What nonsense! If you

feel like that, you can go home – no one's stopping you. I shall stay here all night and make my plans.' The dogs had started barking again and the atmosphere was growing more and more depressing. Then we heard a man shouting and the barking seemed to be coming nearer. Polly jumped up and rushed to the ladder. 'Quick, let's get out of here,' she cried and I heard her jump down the last steps of the ladder. I followed her more slowly, carrying the lantern. I turned it out before I left the barn, then ran into the field, keeping close to the hedge. I heard two men's angry voices and they were definitely making for the barn. They must have seen the light shining through the hole in the wall that I used to pretend was a window. I could hear Polly ahead of me, but it was too dark to see her. She stopped and waited for me and I wondered if she realized she was making for home. We hardly spoke as we walked except to say things like 'Mind that bramble' or 'Take care, there are masses of cowpats here'. All the way I was afraid she would suddenly realize how near home we were and make off and I'd have to face Mother without her. She did show signs of nerves as we entered our ugly little road and stumbled over builders' rubbish. 'I hate this place,' she muttered as she fell over a brick and caught my arm to steady herself. 'Are you sure Aunt Lawrence isn't in the house?' I reassured her and then we were actually walking past the holly hedge and up the tiled path. Mother must have heard our steps, because she opened the door and rushed at Polly, kissing and hugging her as if she had been away for months instead of hours.

Just as I was going to sleep I suddenly found myself laughing. 'Nigel!' I whispered. 'That's just the sort of name Goldy would have . . . Nigel . . .'

Eight

IN SPITE of our late night we all got up early the next morning, except for Polly. Mother insisted on her spending the morning in bed for the obvious purpose of keeping her out of Aunt Lawrence's way. Also her face was in a damaged condition from all the tears that had been shed on it and her poor droopy eyes were almost closed. We told Mrs Hand she had a touch of influenza, practising the lie several times to get used to it before our aunt arrived.

At about ten-thirty she stalked through the gate with a reluctant Ruby trailing behind. We hadn't expected our cousin, and Mother gave her a withering glance, which caused her to start hopping up and down on the doorstep, mumbling: 'Oh dear, I can see I'm not popular here.' Aunt Lawrence didn't get much of a reception either. She eyed Esmé and me coldly and said: 'Why are you girls not at school? I want to talk to your mother privately.' Then she turned to Mother. 'Well, Dora, I have come here this morning at great inconvenience to discuss what we are to do about this daughter of yours.'

She marched into the drawing-room and we all trooped after her. Mother, looking very ill at ease, asked: 'Would you like Mrs Hand to make you some coffee?' Aunt flicked some dust off a chair before she sat on it. 'Of course not, I've only just had breakfast. Now, Dora, don't stall. What are we to do about this unpleasant affair? Please send those girls somewhere else; we cannot discuss this properly with them listening to every word. Where is Polly? Locked in her room, I presume.'

Mother looked at us appealingly, swallowed several times and said with her eyes almost closed: 'I am sorry to say this, Aunt, but I think you are making mountains out of molehills, I really do. Polly admits that she has been for several walks with this boy – Nigel, I think his name is – she also admits that they have smoked cigarettes together, but that is all that has occurred except for a few kisses, no doubt.' She looked hard at Ruby. 'All that rubbish about walking on the towpath with their arms round each other is nonsense.' Ruby, who was standing behind her mother's chair, twisting herself into knots, croaked: 'Perhaps I didn't see clearly. I'm always telling Mother I need spectacles.' Mother continued as if she were reading from a book: 'I agree it was thoughtless and unwise behaviour, but not a crime. The boy is leaving school and joining his parents abroad in a few weeks, and the whole thing will blow over. I can't think why she didn't ask him to the house and avoid all this trouble. Really, Aunt, I must protest about the things you said to Polly last night. They were cruel and wicked things to say to a young girl and I think Uncle Lawrence would agree with me.'

Aunt Lawrence was left almost speechless by this attack. 'Dora,' she cried indignantly, 'how can you turn on me after all I have done for you?'

Mother shrank back in her chair, then almost screamed: 'I'm not turning on you, but I won't have filthy things said about my children. You were enjoying yourself last night, you know you were.' I was glad she hurried from the room at this point before she completely broke down and was bullied into taking back her brave words. Esmé and I exchanged glances as we heard her running up the stairs. This enraged our aunt and she said something about us all being tarred with the same brush, but what could you expect? She let herself out of the front door with Ruby, plucking at her lip, cringing behind. Her parting shot was: 'You should tell that woman to clean the steps, they are disgusting.'

The iron gate banged and they were gone. We saw their heads bobbing past the holly hedge, then we turned to each other and simultaneously burst into unexpected laughter, the sort that won't stop. We leant against the hall walls and laughed until our insides hurt and still we couldn't stop.

As the day went on, Mother began to have qualms about her opposition to Aunt Lawrence and kept asking nervously: 'I wasn't really rude, was I? I can't remember exactly what I said, although I'd learnt it by heart before,' and: 'Perhaps I shouldn't have said she enjoyed saying those things to Polly, but it was true.' We kept telling her how wonderful she had been and how proud we were of her, but a little later she sighed: 'I'm very fond of your uncle, you know. I shall be sorry not to see him any more.'

She need not have worried because, when we were all seated round the dining-room table with our dirty cups and crumby plates before us, we heard the gate slam and, looking through the windows, saw the Lawrences bearing down on us.

'Not twice in one day!' Esmé exclaimed as Polly left the table and tore up to her room. Mother cried: 'What shall I do now? I haven't rehearsed what to say.' To our surprise Uncle Lawrence took off his hat and lightly tapped the window with his stick. His face appeared quite kindly. Esmé, who was the bravest of us, went to the door with Toby trotting after her. Mother left the table and slowly walked towards the hall, whispering to herself and looking as if she was going to the scaffold.

While she was closeted with the Lawrences, I cleared away the tea-things and Esmé went upstairs to Polly: we didn't want her running away again. The usual natter-natter came from the drawing-room with an added rumble from Uncle Lawrence, then his laugh and a little later, to my surprise, Mother's laugh. I joined my sisters upstairs to tell them laughs were actually coming out of the drawing-room and we all sat on the bed with the door open, listening.

Uncle Lawrence: 'So you think we had better not see Polly today. Pity, but perhaps you are right.'

Mother: 'Definitely not today. The poor child has rather a cold.'

Uncle Lawrence: 'Sunday then. Bring her to luncheon on Sunday.'

Aunt Lawrence: 'Good-bye, dear. Sorry I was so hasty, but Ruby made such a bother, silly girl.'

A chorus of good-byes and they were gone.

When the coast was quite clear, we all went down to Mother, and Esmé and I showered her with questions. She was so relieved and happy it made her quite incoherent, but from her disjointed remarks we gathered that Uncle Lawrence ('he really is the dearest man') thought Polly should have a year at a Swiss finishing school and had offered to pay half the expenses ('so very generous of him'). Esmé asked where the other half was coming from. Uncle Lawrence had thought Father's brother Frederick would like to pay for that; Mother, however, did not think he would like it at all. 'He always was the meanest man. I remember when he went on a cruise he took his own deck-chairs,' etc., etc. 'Yes, Mother, we remember about that, but the other half – if Uncle Frederick is too mean to pay it, who will?' we asked. Mother appeared surprised at the question. 'Why, dears, I shall pay it myself, of course.' Then she told us she still had all her jewellery, which she had been keeping to sell in an emergency. She had had in mind a sudden illness, but she realized that education was far more important than illness, since the effects of it lasted just as long. As Mother had not worn her jewellery since Father died, we all thought it had gone in the sale, but now it appeared that she owned two diamond rings that Father had given her and a real pearl necklace which had belonged to her mother and was considered to be valuable – 'and I'll still have a gold brooch and my cornelian bracelet and some other odds and ends,' Mother ended cheerfully, 'and I shan't sell those.'

Polly hadn't said a word. She just sat on the bottom step of the stairs with her eyes fixed on Mother, absent-mindedly pulling pieces of rubber off the soles of her gym shoes. At last she said: 'I don't know what to make of all this. Is it meant to be a punishment? Why should I be the one to have this chance? I don't know if I would like to go or not, because I can't suddenly imagine how it would be in a Swiss school.' She stood up and went to Mother shyly. 'Your jewellery, Mother – you mustn't sell it to send me away. I could get a job as a mother's help if necessary.'

A look of pain passed over Mother's face. 'My darling, we are not sending you away as a punishment. It's a reward because you have worked so hard and had so few pleasures lately.'

We spent the entire evening discussing Polly's future life in a Swiss school. There was much to discuss – clothes, language difficulties, dates and the danger of growing a goitre. 'I believe everyone gets one sooner or later in Switzerland,' Mother said knowledgeably; 'but you could always wear a necklace to hide the scar.'

The Lawrences obtained brochures of various Swiss finishing schools and we pored over them. It was a queer thing:

Aunt Lawrence always became kind after she had been particularly beastly. It was as if it took the poison out of her. Now she was continually coming round with lengths of material and paper patterns and French dictionaries. There was a bit of unpleasantness one day about corsets. She was insisting that Polly took two pairs of boned corsets with her – 'otherwise you will spread', but Polly, remembering how Ruby and Grace moaned about their corsets, flatly refused. Mrs Hand joined in and said with great emphasis that Polly's stomach would come out in a point after she had had some children if she wasn't careful of it now. But Polly was firm and corsets were crossed off the list.

Nine

MOTHER'S JEWELLERY was sold and part of it was
turned into a young lady's school wardrobe. Polly was to
have a new trunk, a hat-box and a special box for gloves. A
dressmaker came every day and made underclothing, and
the night-dresses had ribbon threaded through them, and the
camisoles were embroidered with scalloped edging. We were
all so enthusiastic about this trousseau it was almost as if
Polly was getting married. The school that had been chosen
was at Montreux: it looked a beautiful place from the
brochure, with its dining-hall with long refectory tables and
bowls of fruit on them, even containing pineapples, its
chintzy sitting-rooms and its dormitories with large windows
looking on to incredibly lovely scenery. The girls seemed
more like hotel visitors than school girls. Sometimes Polly
felt afraid of going to this school and at other times she
couldn't wait to get there. She took out her old school-books
and studied French and, when John came home for the holidays, he helped her, but Mother said their French did not
sound quite right, although it was a long time since she had
heard any. It was only on the last two days before Polly
was due to leave us that we realized she was really going
away. The sight of the half-filled trunks and boxes depressed

us dreadfully and Toby even put his head into one and wept. Although we had complained about Polly managing us so firmly, now she was going we felt afraid to be without her, and Mother kept saying she didn't know how she would manage. Esmé and I felt as if a great weight of responsibility were about to descend on our shoulders and wished we were being sent to Switzerland as well.

Polly left on my eleventh birthday, but a birthday seemed a small thing compared with Polly's departure. She was to be accompanied as far as Victoria by Uncle Lawrence. We saw them off on the windy station and all Polly could think of was what on earth she could talk about on the journey: 'Two and a half hours shut up in a little railway carriage with him. We are travelling first, so it won't be crowded. I've never cared for horses and now I'll have to talk to one for the whole journey.' I think our uncle was as scared of talking to Polly as she was of talking to him. He hurried to the bookstall and returned with the *Bystander* and the *Windsor* magazine, handing them to her as if she were a pretty woman. She almost was, and we were proud of her as she walked with us up and down the platform, wearing her well-cut grey coat and little round navy-blue hat. Her bushy fair hair was neatly tied back with an enormous, stiff navy-blue ribbon and, with her glowing cheeks, she looked awfully wholesome, like an advertisement for some patent food. As the express bore her away, we stood in a disconsolate group, but John, watching wistfully, said: 'How I envy her crossing the Channel and travelling through France and Switzerland.' Mother agreed, but added: 'Poor child, I hope she won't be sick. The first time I crossed the Channel I was sick in your father's umbrella; by mistake, of course.'

For the first few days after Polly left us we were in a frightful muddle. The mornings started off badly because no one got up at the right time: we lay in bed waiting to hear

Polly running downstairs and the sound of her raking out the range. None of us knew how to light the range or cope with things called dampers, so the breakfast was cooked on an oil stove we always referred to as 'Old Smeller'. Fortunately the porridge was cooked in a double saucepan and we couldn't burn it. Then there was the shopping. We tried to do some of it on the way back from school, but forgot what Mother had asked us to buy. For some reason she would not carry a basket, because there were people in the town who had known her as a girl. 'It wouldn't do, dears. Perhaps a basket containing flowers or fruit or even mushrooms, but carrots, potatoes and kippers – I couldn't. Polly would insist on us dealing with those cheap shops where there is no delivery.' When she suggested dealing with more expensive shops, Esmé wisely said that we must keep on with the old ones: 'You know what you will be like, Mother, when you get into a shop filled with delicious things; you just won't be able to resist them. It would be cheaper for Mrs Hand to do the shopping, even if it means her coming for an extra hour.'

So Mrs Hand came for three hours every day and then it had to be four, and still things didn't run smoothly. Mother tried to teach the little ones, but as often as not forgot, and it was decided that Clare would have to attend the high school the following term, which pleased her very much. 'Will they have singing lessons?' she kept asking, and we hardly liked to tell her how disgusting the singing lessons were: about thirty girls with fifteen books, nearly all singing the most revolting songs completely out of tune, songs about Spring, Spring, SPRING and roaming over the downs so free.

Very occasionally women came and called on Mother and asked her out to luncheon, never to dinner. If Esmé or I were included in the invitation and if it was a Saturday, we had to go, although it ruined our holiday. I remember being dragged off on a lovely May morning to have luncheon at the dark house of a miserable old solicitor who had recently re-married. His wife was fairly young, a distant connection of his first wife, and I was surprised at how she had managed to brighten up the house without exactly doing anything to it. Some of the heavy curtains had gone, there were flowers in all the rooms, and the stuffy smell of old soup and must had gone too. The solicitor was away for a few days and, although his gentle bride did not say so, it was easy to see it was a rest for her. I had heard that he was an extremely mean man and that, when his daughter had lived at home many years ago, she used to steal flowers from the garden and sell them on the station. I thought this romantic until I saw Annie, a middle-aged, rabbit-faced spinster who kept house for an aged aunt in Bournemouth.

We had to wait some time for luncheon because there was another guest, a Mrs Alexander, who had spent a lot of her life in Italy. Our hostess told me I wasn't to be surprised if she appeared a little eccentric, but she had a heart of gold and had rendered our hostess a great service some years ago. 'She lives a completely retired life now and sees no one. Even I am not allowed to call on her, although she occasionally visits me.'

When at last the guest arrived, she was far more eccentric than I had expected; in fact she was like no human being I had ever seen before. It was difficult to keep my eyes off her because she had a kind of ravaged, fabulous beauty like some old and exotic doll in a museum, glittering and dusty. She wore a mauve silk turban on her head, and her hair – the little I could see – was cropped and dyed an astonishing purple-red. Her eyes in her deathly white face were large and very beautiful, a sort of mauve-blue, exactly the colour of periwinkles. Her face was tiny and delicate, but withered, although she was not old. She gave the impression that she was about to break and crumble away. Wrapped round her slender body was a fantastic black and white coat with long fur hanging from the bottom. But the strangest thing of all was her golden, pointed slippers. Later I was to learn that they were repainted every day by her chauffeur. As soon as Mrs Alexander entered the room, she ran up to our hostess and kissed her on both cheeks, apologizing for being so late, and if one had not seen how derelict she was, it might have been a pretty young girl speaking with a slight foreign accent. Her voice was charming.

I sat opposite her at the luncheon-table and I could not help looking at her more than I should. She still wore her coat wrapped round her, which was annoying because I was longing to see what she wore underneath. She ate little, only using her fork, and I had the impression she was not comfortable eating at such a massive table. I could imagine her nibbling tiny meals from a tray on her lap. I think Mother was as fascinated by her as I was and we both spoke little, just listening to Mrs Alexander's pretty chatter occasionally interrupted by soothing remarks from our hostess. It appeared that she was taking piano lessons, hoped to give concerts in the near future, and had recently bought a concert grand piano and was now having trouble because there was a large amount of money owing for it. The firm had threatened to take it away, but, when some men arrived with a great van and a trolly to wheel it out of the house, they found it impossible to remove because she had made the music-room in the cellars of her house and had the wall rebuilt after the piano was installed. She was immensely pleased about this and kept giving malicious chuckles. She said that she would, of course, pay for the piano when she was playing professionally.

There was a lot about monkeys: her house was full of

them. And she had once kept a bear, but people had complained because it used to break into church during the services, and it had to be given to a zoo. 'I sometimes wonder why I ever returned to England, so many unpleasant things happen here.'

When we were about to leave the house, Mrs Alexander offered to drive us home in her motor-car. We walked down the dark stone steps together and a servant opened the heavy gates and we were in the sunlight outside. The car was not at all the kind of car I had expected to see. It was a queer little open one, painted vivid yellow, and the bonnet sloped downwards as if someone had given it a great bang with a heavy mallet. There was a seedy-looking chauffeur sitting at the wheel, looking as if he had been cut out of tin. Mother and I squeezed into the back seat. Mrs Alexander sat with the chauffeur in front and, when she had wrapped some chiffon scarves round her head and shoulders, we jerked off. Perhaps the tyres were too full of air or there was something wrong with the springs, but we bounced about the road in the most extraordinary way and had to hold on to our seats in danger of being shot over the low sides of the car. Feeling a little sick, we were delivered safely to the gate of The Hollies. Just as the car was driving off, Mrs Alexander leant out and called to Mother: 'I'd like to see more of your daughter. You have no objection, I hope?' Surprised, Mother replied wildly:

'Oh no, none at all. I have six of them you know, girls and boys.'

When she had driven away, Mother exclaimed: 'I wouldn't have missed meeting her for anything. Aren't you pleased you came, dear?' It certainly had been a more interesting luncheon than usual, but I was not sure that I wanted to see that queer woman again.

Polly wrote home every week. At first she seemed a little

bewildered and homesick, and the thought that she was to stay at school for the summer holidays weighed on her mind. Then other girls' names started to appear in her letters. 'Crystal and I are learning to row on the lake' or 'A German girl called Freda is teaching me German. I think I would like to take up languages seriously.' There were references to picture galleries, museums, a clock factory and picnics. 'I don't tell anyone I find the concerts boring. You know I never cared for music much and now I find I shall have to sit through a whole opera one evening next month. You can't believe how my dancing has improved, and my hands. I have delicate, almond-shaped nails now.' It was no longer the bossy Polly of the kitchen. It was strange how completely she appeared to have forgotten Goldy. It saddened me, because it seemed so unromantic to forget him like that. After the Lawrences had made such a dreadful fuss about him, Mother actually told Polly she could ask him to the house if she liked, so that she could see him before he left school. But Polly had refused and said gruffly that she never wanted to see him again. I believe she wrote him a formal note saying she would be unable to meet him any more. Sometimes in the darkness of our bedroom I would discuss the situation with Esmé and I suggested that Goldy had proposed to Polly and she had refused him. But she said: 'I expect the thought of him makes her feel sick.' Esmé had lost her interest in proposals and we no longer read them out loud to each other.

For some time I only saw Ruby at Sunday luncheons and she kept looking away and swallowing when any of our family were about. I knew that she felt guilty and miserable for spying on Polly, and months later she explained her behaviour to me: 'You see, Mother is only nice to me when I tell her things, then afterwards she sometimes turns on me. I may have been mistaken when I said Polly and that dreadful boy had their arms round one another, but Mother listened so eagerly that it made me say more than I meant. I didn't want to do Polly any harm, but I wanted to please Mother.' Then more brightly: 'Well, it has all turned out for the best, you must admit that. Anyway, it's no good crying over spilt milk.'

Poor Ruby, she had taken to wearing an enormous hat turned up on one side like Australians wear, to balance her nose, she said. She still spent some time with Vanda at the farm when she could escape from home and sometimes I met her there. Once I saw her coming away from the farm crying. When she saw me, she started dabbing at her little eyes with a spotted handkerchief and pretended that dust had blown into them. She told me I had better keep away from Vanda: 'She's in a terrible temper. Something to do with the Major, I think, but she was dreadfully rude to me; in fact she called me a cow, and that is the worst thing you can call a woman – you are too young to understand, but it is so. She seemed as if she had been drinking and I'm beginning to think Mother is right about her.'

We walked through the fields together, but she wouldn't let me stop to pick the moon-daisies because of damaging the grass, which was intended for her father's hay. It was the first time that year that I was wearing summer clothes and I felt so free and light that I had to run ahead, waving my bare arms about as if I was flying. Ruby trudged behind on her thin, rat-like feet, holding her great hat in one hand and swinging a bulky black bag with the other.

After Polly went away, the butcher was always calling at the house for orders. Mother said it saved her walking all the way to the shop and she did not trust Mrs Hand to buy meat, as she was quite capable of buying Canterbury lamb. Canterbury lamb sounded delicious, but apparently it was about the last thing decent people allowed in their larders.

Instead of the fish-paste and cheese sandwiches we used to take to school, we now had ones with big lumps of meat inside and we found them more sustaining. The effects of the other sandwiches only lasted about an hour, then we were hungry again. 'It must be all this growing we are doing,' Esmé used to say as our insides rumbled in a hollow way when we walked home from school. Esmé certainly was growing rapidly. She was as tall as Mother already and as slender as a hollyhock. But I was growing far more slowly and I had a sad feeling that I was going to be stumpy when I grew up, or even squat, and I earnestly hoped that all this meat I was eating would increase my height. I did not want people to think I was kneeling instead of standing.

One Saturday morning Mother kept fussing because the joint hadn't been delivered, and eventually Esmé and I trudged resentfully to the town, grumbling all the way about wasting our Saturday morning. We looked into the blacksmith's as we passed and were amused to see that he was shoeing a very elegant little donkey – it had never occurred to us that donkeys wore horse-shoes and we wondered if they were lucky. We wasted quite a lot of time at the forge, but the blacksmith was used to us because we used to stop and warm our hands there in winter. We even liked the smell of burning hoofs and sometimes burnt our finger-nails against the hot range at home and sniffed the same smell.

We had to wait our turn in the butcher's shop, squashed by women with huge shoulders and no necks and cheeky maid-servants in print dresses. When it was our turn to be served, everyone listened to our order. Esmé asked for a shoulder of best lamb and two pounds of rump steak and added that the boy had not called at our house for days. The butcher asked our name and said crossly: 'I thought as much. Tell your mother there will be no more meat until she settles her bill,' adding more kindly: 'Sorry, ducks, but there it is. We have all got to live, you know.' Everyone was looking at us and someone said: 'Poor kids,' which made it more awful, but Esmé replied quite calmly: 'I will tell my mother what you say. It must be an oversight.'

We had to push past the women as we left the shop and, although we could feel their eyes burning into us, we walked away slowly, saying silly things to each other like: 'I hope this weather lasts,' until we were out of sight. We ran the rest of the way home and, banging open the front door, shouted: 'Mother – the butcher. He won't let us have any more meat until you have paid the bill.' To our surprise Mother was fairly calm about it. She fiddled with the knob on the end of the blind cord and said disdainfully: 'How absurd! What can you expect when the man is a Liberal?' Esmé suggested that, even if he was a Conservative, he would want his money. Mother turned away from the window and answered with a weary smile: 'But he would wait for it like a gentleman,' then she went upstairs to fetch her hat and gloves. When she came down a few minutes later she was wearing a black dress and black chiffon hat decorated with one large rose. 'It's a pity it's too warm to wear my fur coat,' she murmured to herself as she adjusted her gloves; then briskly: 'Esmé, I'm afraid you will have to come with me to carry the basket.' Esmé made a face, but went off without a protest – she often surprised me by her bravery – and some time later they returned, Esmé carrying a well-filled basket. Mother said: 'Take the steak in to Mrs Hand and tell her to prepare it for luncheon. It will be late today, I'm afraid.' She trailed upstairs and I turned to Esmé and asked her how they had managed to bring all this meat home. Had they gone to another butcher? 'Oh no,' Esmé said tiredly, 'we went to the Liberal butcher, but Mother sort of dazzled him and he left all his customers to bow us into the street when we left. She was very haughty with him, you know, talking about estates being wound up, whatever that means. She did mention the Lawrences as well.'

It was just after the trouble with the butcher that we met Mrs Alexander and heard about the men coming to take the piano away because she had not paid for it. I was beginning to feel sorry for tradesmen. I asked a girl at school, whose father sold horses' harness and other things made of leather, if he had many customers who failed to pay their bills. She said he certainly had, and some of them were the richest people in the neighbourhood. She became quite excited about all the people who owed her father money and I was afraid in case the Lawrences were included amongst them and tried to change the subject, without much success. Another girl, whose father owned a large draper's shop, joined in the conversation and said that he often had to resort to taking out summonses before customers paid their debts, and they did not always even then. I asked if their fathers were Liberals because my mother had told me only Liberals dunned people for money. The draper's daughter laughed, showing a great many pointed teeth, and said her father was a Tory member of the Council and he didn't care whom he summoned, although he usually warned them first. She admitted that the richer the customer appeared, the longer credit he gave. I remarked that he wouldn't give my family much credit, because we were about as poor as we could be. 'In that case,' she laughed, 'I don't expect he would allow you any. Perhaps he would if he knew that you were a friend of mine,' she added kindly.

I repeated this conversation to Mother, who said crossly: 'I wish you wouldn't talk to tradesmen's daughters; there must be some girls with decent backgrounds in the school. Also you must not go about saying we are poor. It will ruin my credit.'

Esmé had recently made friends with a brewer's daughter and, although he was a tradesman, nothing was said about it. The Bowmans lived in a large red house the other side of the town and their stables contained four hunters and two ponies. They encouraged Esmé to use one of the ponies as much as she liked, and they even allowed her to call it her pony and let her change its name from Trixie to Tempest. Almost every evening Esmé would rush off to the Bowmans, and Saturday afternoons as well, so I was alone more than usual. I loved the little ones, but they were too young for us to have much in common, and I had not been near Vanda since she had called Ruby a cow. I would not have minded being called a cow much, but I was afraid of Vanda's tempers. I had seen her in them several times and found them terrifying, although they had not been directed at me so far. The farm-boys were usually the victims. Sometimes they left the back door open and let hens get into the house or made a noise and disturbed Jane when she was asleep. Sometimes she accused them of stealing her cigarettes. It was really just the mood she was in – she was quite capable of making them cups of tea and sitting on the kitchen table gossiping with them while they drank it.

It must have been the Saturday after I had first met Mrs Alexander that she came to take me away. I was sitting rather disconsolately under our tree, watching Toby unwind the insides of a golf ball he had found. 'I don't know what I'm going to do with all this stuff,' he said contentedly as he stuffed elastic into his pocket, 'but it's bound to come in useful some day.'

Clare was peering through a hole in the fence and reporting what she saw: 'There's a dog running about with a whole lot of friends following. Here's that old woman who always wears a hat like a currant bun and she's carrying a live hen upside down. Oh, and here's a funny little yellow car with a

fairy godmother sitting beside the chauffeur, no, it's a witch.'
I left the shady tree and went to peer through the hole, pushing Clare away. I was just in time to see Mrs Alexander
being assisted from the car by the chauffeur. Although the
day was warm, she was still wearing the coat with the long
fur hanging from the hem, but her turban was different, a
blue one this time, and she had matching sapphire ear-rings
in her ears. She flitted up our path, her pointed gold slippers
hardly seeming to touch the ground. I ran into the house
and, as I reached the hall, I saw Mother opening the front
door and heard Mrs Alexander say: 'I've come to take your
daughter Frances away.' Mother, rather startled, said: 'Oh,
have you? Er, not for long I hope.' They went into the
drawing-room and I followed, feeling slightly afraid. Mrs
Alexander was standing with her back to the window adjusting her turban with her little, claw-like hand. She smiled at
me in a very pretty way and said she had come to borrow
me for the day because she was feeling lonely. I said I'd like
to spend the day with her because I was feeling lonely too.
This appeared to please her and she took my hand and said
we were going to be great friends; she had had a little girl
once, but she had died when she was three. 'I will show you
my darling's portrait when we get home. She would be about
your age if she had lived. No, perhaps a little older.'

Mother wanted me to change my dress, which had lost its
freshness, but Mrs Alexander said it was charming, she loved
gingham, even when it was a little soiled.

I sat in the back of the car with Mrs Alexander while we
bounced about so much it was difficult to talk. In spite of
the jolting she wore a grand air, with her head thrown back
and her huge eyes half closed. She was watching everything
though, because to my horror she suddenly started chanting
to a most inoffensive-looking woman scuttling along the
pavement: 'Silly little mustard-pot, silly little mustard-pot,

wouldn't you like a little mustard-pot?' The woman disappeared into a shop and Mrs Alexander laughed. 'Silly bitch, I was very kind to her at one time, nursed her when she was ill, when we quarrelled over her damn-fool maid. Said I bribed her with drink to make her gossip. I did too, and still do.' She gave her glittering laugh. 'Called my car a silly little mustard-pot, but she was glad enough to drive in it.' Although Mrs Alexander's ex-friend ignored her, other people didn't and several pedestrians turned and gazed at the car and its owner with astonishment; others laughed and I was relieved when we turned down a side street. The chauffeur just drove on and I began to think he was deaf and dumb, since I'd never heard him utter a word.

I imagined that Mrs Alexander would live in a strange, dark old house, and was surprised when we turned into a suburban street of neat gabled houses with churchy gates and flowering shrubs in their front gardens. The car stopped in front of a house that did not look as clean as the others: the windows were dirty and the curtains made of ragged orange net. There is something awfully depressing about grimy orange, far worse than dirty white. An old greyhound with a goitre growing from its neck slowly got up from the front-door step and gave us a mournful welcome and slowly lay down again. We had to step over it to get into the house.

Although it was early summer, there was a fire burning in the hall, and some low chairs and a small mother-of-pearl table were arranged in front of it. A grey parrot was chained to a perch and kept shouting: 'Antonio, Antonio' as soon as the door was opened, then relapsed into silence. The chauffeur followed us into the hall, carrying several black mackintosh bags containing bread, old cabbages and other food for the animals, and trailed off to the kitchen to prepare it. 'Don't forget to take off your white coat, Povey,'

Mrs Alexander shouted after him. Then, turning her great eyes on me, she asked what I would like to do. I immediately said I would like to see the monkeys, which was the main reason I had come. I had never known anyone who had monkeys living in the house before.

There was a conservatory leading from the hall, where all the animals lived and died. They didn't smell as much as they might have, but they were not at all attractive. They were kept in cages and boxes – monkeys, listless kittens, rabbits and doves and, I think, a few guinea-pigs as well. None of them looked happy. Mrs Alexander took a pretty yellow-greenish monkey out of its cage, which climbed on to her shoulder and gazed at me with its sad eyes while she talked to it in Italian. It suddenly made a grab at one of her ear-rings, nearly tearing her ear, so it was put back in its cage while she unhooked her ear-rings. She wanted me to hold it, but I did not like the look of its damp, sticky hands and turned my attention to some tortoises which were clumping round the tiled floor. Then I noticed some charming green frogs in a glass box, as vivid and shiny as if they were made of enamel and very delicately formed. She told me they were Italian tree-frogs: she had only had them a few days and already one had escaped. There were four monkeys altogether, and I did not like any of them as much as I had expected. It was partly seeing them with the kittens and rabbits. One kitten had an eye missing and I was sure a monkey had pulled it out.

When we left the animals, I asked if I could see the garden, because I was longing to smell some fresh air. Mrs Alexander was surprised and said there was nothing in the garden to see because that fool Povey didn't look after it properly. She suggested showing me her music-room under the ground instead. We had to pass through the garden to get there and I could see what she meant about it. It was just dried-up earth decorated with a few weeds and patches of long grass in the shadowy parts. There was a small stone statue of a cupid, which she evidently prized because she had tied an umbrella over its head to protect it from the sun and rain.

We went down a narrow staircase and Mrs Alexander unlocked a black door with a monkey painted on it and we entered the music-room. It must have been made in the foundations of the house and it had no windows, in spite of which it was a lovely room and not at all dreary. The walls were painted white and hung with unframed oil paintings, some of monkeys which she had painted herself, others more professional-looking, painted in vivid colours like no pictures I had seen before. There was one that appealed to me particularly because it had captured the colours that appear on wet roads that have had oil spilt on them: she said it was painted by a young Jew called Mark Gertler and would be valuable one day. The others were by her dead husband; she expected they would have to be sold soon to pay for her music lessons. I was so interested in the paintings that I had forgotten about the music and only then noticed the concert-sized grand piano that had not been paid for.

While I had been looking at the paintings, Mrs Alexander had lit the fire, which was already laid. Then, after washing her hands in a small basin in a corner of the room, she sat down at the piano and asked if I would like to hear her play. 'Do you care for Beethoven, dear?' she asked. I said I did, although I couldn't remember hearing any, then I remembered my mother used to play something she told us was Beethoven's farewell to the piano, written after he went completely deaf, so I asked for that. She said she would play the Moonlight Sonata because she had not heard of the piece I mentioned, and I was glad she hadn't because the Moonlight Sonata was wonderful. I curled up in a chair and

117

listened with a deep and delicious pleasure – it was as if I was ears and nothing else. It was more like lapping water than moonlight and I was drowning in it.

Mrs Alexander must have played to me for about two hours, and when we came up from the bowels of the earth the sky had clouded. It was almost as if it were another day. We sat beside the hall fire and Povey brought us a tray of tea. There was no milk served with the tea, only slices of lemon, but there were chocolate biscuits that had been specially bought for me. Mrs Alexander did not make embarrassing conversation for children, perhaps she did not know how, she just said anything that came into her head – how she had turned cartwheels all over a hotel floor an hour before her daughter was born, how she had run away from her finishing school and ridden horses in circuses, and how poor she and her husband had sometimes been, not a dull sort of poverty like ours, but a wandering-over-the-face-of-the-earth kind. Once they had tried pig-farming in Australia and the pigs had been fed on peaches, another time she had worked as a maternity nurse in a Paris hospital. Eventually the husband's paintings had started to sell for high prices and they had settled in Italy, where he had been persistently unfaithful to her and she had run away several times – always with other men, though. She told me malicious things about her neighbours; they were people I'd never met, so it did not matter. She was not on speaking terms with those next door because they complained to the police when two of her monkeys climbed through the nursery window and frightened their children. She sat there talking in her pretty voice with its slight foreign accent, holding her tea-cup in both hands and still wrapped in her black and white coat. I had a glimpse of what was underneath it – a sort of skin-tight black dress as far as I could make out. She was a queer colour when you had a good look at her. Perhaps it

118

was because she put permanganate of potash in her bath, which, she said, was why her hair was purple-red. She kept it cropped short and covered it with her chiffon turbans of all colours, threaded with gold and silver.

After my first visit, Mrs Alexander often sent the car for me and sometimes, when the sun was shining, I did not want to go at all. I never tired of her playing the piano. Now I look back on it I realize that she was a poor pianist, slap-dash and showy, but I had heard so little music that it seemed perfect to me, and often tears poured down my round cheeks as I listened. I found her conversation fascinating too, except when it became too queer and frightening. It was the un-healthy, enclosed feeling of the house I didn't care for. I found the imprisoned animals distressing too. They frequently died, and Mrs Alexander used to carry out post-mortem examinations on their bodies, fortunately not when I was around. She always said they died of liver or fatty heart or some human sort of illness, but I felt their deaths were due to the monkey's mischievous, damp hands.

Usually the car came to take me away on Saturday mornings, which meant I would have luncheon with her. She almost lived on tomato soup out of little blue packets, which I thought was delicious, although it did not taste in the least like tomato soup, more like cheap sweets. We ate out of bowls on our laps, huddling round the hall fire. We even ate fish out of bowls. The fish was horrible, baked and served with the fishy water it had been cooked in. I don't think she ever ate meat or ordinary meals.

One Saturday morning when she sent the little yellow car for me I was not at home because I had gone to Vanda's farm. When I got there one of the men told me she was away on a visit to her mother, but I still hung about because I didn't want to spend the day shut up in Mrs Alexander's house. The farmer showed me the poor blind bull bellowing in a shed and was surprised that I didn't enjoy looking at it. Then he showed me something I liked much better, some baby bantams, very small and perfect, and gave me four bantam's eggs to take home, one for each of us children. I carried them carefully through the fields, two in each hand. I was glad I had stayed out so long because Mrs Alexander had sent her dreadful little car for me and it had waited for almost an hour.

Ten

IT HAD BEEN my turn to have luncheon with the Lawrences. When we were drinking our coffee in the room like a conservatory where the birds lived, Aunt Lawrence abruptly broke off a discussion she was having with my uncle about selling some horses to the police force and turned to Mother accusingly to say: 'What is all this about Frances driving about in an open car with that mad Italian woman?'

I was on the point of leaving the room with Grace to look at some hurdles that had been put up for her to practise jumping over, but we paused at the door to hear Mother's reply. 'Has she?' she said, opening her eyes wide. 'Oh yes, of course; Mrs Alexander. The child enjoys listening to her playing the piano, you know. I don't think the woman's mad, only eccentric.'

Aunt Lawrence put down her coffee-cup and said firmly: 'I have never met the woman, but I have seen her driving about in a tin-pot motor-car looking as mad as a hatter. Wears a turban, doesn't pay her bills, plays at being a nurse, keeps unlimited monkeys and paints her slippers gold. Of course the woman isn't sane.' Mother bit her lip and started twisting her handkerchief like a child, then asked: 'Do you think I should not let Frances see her any more then? I don't think she will do the child any harm, although she does talk so wildly. I must admit I found her fascinating, so original and amusing.'

Ruby interrupted her by saying: 'Mrs Jenkins who lives in Walnut Cottage was only telling me the other day that Mrs Alexander hardly ever pays her chauffeur's wages and she hit him once because he broke a plate. It wasn't the plate she minded about, but the noise it made breaking on the kitchen floor. Oh, and Mother, Mrs Jenkins said you are quite right about that girl in the post office who married the bank clerk. She *had* to get married. To think that she was handing out stamps only a week or two ago!'

Grace and I left the room at this point because we found Ruby's stories so self-righteous and boring. The hurdles in the paddock were boring too, just sticks of various heights – I had expected there would be water like they have at some of the jumps at horse-shows. Then Grace took me into the barn to show me some butterfly-trimmed cami-knickers she was wearing, the first I had seen. She said they were difficult to go to the lavatory in, but all the same I would have liked a pair myself, even if they made me constipated. She also told me that Charles was returning home soon. He had been away for over a year, six months in Belgium and six months in America staying with relations. The family was very pleased about his return, Ruby in particular, because she hoped he would take her to dances. 'He took her to a hunt ball once and had to dance with her practically the whole evening because no one else would; I'm sure I shall never be a wallflower like poor old Ruby,' Grace said, and started waltzing round the barn. 'Oh, I'm so longing to go to balls. I shan't wear a silly white dress for my coming-out dance, pink perhaps or black. It would be marvellous to come out in black and horrify all the old matrons.' She stopped dancing and said sadly: 'You will never be able to go to a ball now you are so poor, but perhaps you will get asked to small dances in private houses.' Then spitefully: 'I expect you will all go to the hops in the village hall and dance with people's gardeners.'

I looked at her pretty, flushed face and noticed that her teeth were uneven and her nose freckled. This pleased me immensely and I said: 'You'll have to do something about your teeth and those freckles before you go to balls, they notice dreadfully.'

Grace put her hands to her mouth and ran a finger over her teeth and asked worriedly if they really did look awful. I assured her they did and that they seemed to be growing worse every time I saw her, and, although I knew I was being mean, I couldn't help suggesting she had them pulled out and replaced by false ones. Grace cried wildly: 'I'd rather be dead. I'll wear a band, anything rather than have a mouth filled with china teeth. The dentist recommended that I should wear a band, but I pleaded with Mother that I didn't want to wear one. The corsets are bad enough. They dig into my stomach every time I bend down and a plate will dig into my mouth every time I eat, but I'll wear one even if it is torture.'

I was feeling guilty as we left the straw-smelling barn and came out into the bright afternoon. I looked at Grace's depressed face and searched in my mind for something cheerful to say: 'Look, Grace, about your freckles. They really look awfully attractive, sort of summery. They only come on fine skins, not tough ones like mine.' Grace answered crossly: 'I'm not worried about the freckles, they go away in the winter anyway, but you are right about my skin. It is fine. I'm glad I haven't rosy milkmaid's cheeks like you, although they look quite nice on a child.' We walked back to the house together without saying another word, Grace feeling

123

her teeth pensively and I thinking that it was no wonder that the Lawrence family were so spiteful; it was dreadfully catching and gave one such a feeling of power.

The following Saturday, when Mrs Alexander came to collect me, Mother stayed in her bedroom because she was afraid to meet her under the shadow of Aunt Lawrence's disapproval, yet also afraid to forbid me to go to her house. I wouldn't have minded much if she had, although I still enjoyed listening to Mrs Alexander pounding away at her piano. It sounded particularly exciting heard from the garden, as if it was coming up through the earth, but it was not worth the feeling of being frightened and faintly disgusted. I felt guilty listening to her stories, as if I'd been doing something dirty. She told me that women killed their babies before they were born and about a mad sister of hers who came to stay and mooed like a cow all the time. When people complained about the noise she shut her up in the cellar, which was now the music-room. I liked it when she told me about her childhood in India and how she and her two sisters used to gallop on their horses, their long hair of different shades of gold flying out behind them, and about their beautiful mother, who used to take drugs and fall asleep at dinner parties and who suffered from asthma, the result of being left on a marble floor during an earthquake when she was a baby. I think the mother was half Italian, but I never got it quite clear. I knew that both Mrs Alexander's sisters were married to Italians and she sometimes talked about her Italian nephews and nieces. The nephew was the son of her mad sister and had stayed with her fairly recently, but they had not got on at all well after the first week. He said he was starved and used to buy six eggs a day and drink them raw from the shells and prowl round the town after girls. The niece was everything that was lovely except that she suffered from peculiar spots on her face when she was nervous. A whole crop of them came up on her wedding day, but Mrs Alexander had been able to disguise them in some miraculous way and, when she stood at the altar with her young husband, she looked beautiful.

I longed to see photographs of these fascinating relations, but the only photograph she ever showed me was of her dead daughter. She had turned her dirty orange drawing-room into a sort of shrine to this child and had made an altar decorated with tall candles in tarnished candlesticks, dead flowers in Indian bowls, three dark rosaries made of different woods and, in the centre, the photograph of a chubby little girl with her hands folded under her chin and her eyes turning up as if in mock prayer. Poor child, she looked a little horror, most likely due to the Italian photographer, but it made me embarrassed to look at her. The frame was all gilt squirls and whorls, with a separate glass compartment containing a lock of the dead child's hair. In the photograph it appeared very dark, but the framed hair was a brilliant gold, though I did not like to mention this discrepancy. Povey was never allowed to contaminate the drawing-room, which was cleaned about once a fortnight by Mrs Alexander wearing special clothes consisting of a nurse's uniform, a white turban and a crucifix attached to her belt. She considered it a great treat for me to be allowed to help her. I had to wear a table napkin on my head because she considered the room a holy place, but it didn't appear at all holy to me, just dusty and tawdry, with its gilt furniture, artificial flowers and chalky plaster figures of Joseph and Mary. There was one charming thing in the room, but I was not allowed to touch it because it had belonged to this dead child – a brightly painted little donkey-cart from Sicily. The donkey had feathers coming out of its head, or it may have been the driver.

There was another most extraordinary room in Mrs

Alexander's house. The door was always kept locked and I imagined it as unfurnished and full of trunks and things. Then one day she said I could help her clean her surgery and unlocked the door. We went into a room that must have been intended for a dining-room because it had a heavy dining-room sort of air, you could almost smell old joints. The walls were darkly panelled in imitation wood and there was a large alabaster bowl hanging from the ceiling that lit up with gas. But really it was a sort of surgery, with white enamel tables and a lot of enamel bowls of all sizes and shapes heaped in the middle of the room where the dining-room table should have been. There were no curtains, just transparent paper stuck over the windows, the kind they have in cheap lavatories. Apparently Mrs Alexander had once set up as a nurse but had not been allowed to continue her practice for some reason, perhaps because she was not fully qualified. She was convinced that she would be allowed to nurse again some day and every now and again, when she thought of it, she would boil all her instruments. What she really longed to do was operate on someone, but fortunately had never had the chance except for the post-mortems on her dead animals. Sometimes she looked longingly at the goitre on the old greyhound's neck. She had a few diagrams of unskinned people on the walls and a medicine cupboard filled with used bottles and bursting packets, glass and rubber tubes and dried poppy heads. Nothing in it looked as if it would make an ill person feel better.

Sometimes a doctor called to give Mrs Alexander injections and she screamed and screamed as he did it. Now that I have had injections myself, I can't think what all the fuss was about. Once she told me to speak to the doctor as he came downstairs. I was to say: 'Why do you hurt her so much? Please don't hurt her.' I tried to say it, but it stuck in my throat – it was the sort of thing which that dead child in the drawing-room would have said. So I gave the doctor a reproachful glance and hoped that would show him how cruel I thought him.

After a day spent in Mrs Alexander's house, it was a relief to get home to the big sunny kitchen smelling of steak and kidney pie and the sound of the children's voices as they played in the garden and the clink-clink of Mother beating eggs. Esmé would return from a day spent with the Bowmans, her sallow face flushed from riding and her eyes shining even more than usual. 'Hallo, old Frances. Have you spent the day listening to that old witch playing music in her cellar? Do you know the Bowmans have some heavenly spaniel puppies, black and white with the most floppy ears imaginable. I do wish we could have one.'

Esmé seemed full of life, while after a day spent with Mrs Alexander I felt all grey as if I'd been rubbed in ashes. I longed for something to sever my connection with her. I asked Mother if I could hide when Povey came to fetch me and she said: 'Yes dear, if you like,' but when Saturday morning came I dared not. I felt Mrs Alexander would do something terrible to me if I did, climb in through the window and operate on me when I was asleep, or camp outside our house with all her monkeys, or shout awful words after me in the street as she drove past in her motor-car.

One Saturday morning I did dare to visit Vanda, who had been away. She had spent part of the time in France and had returned radiant. Jane was looking much better, although she was still backward in walking. Although I had not seen her for some time, she still remembered me and clung round my neck and did not want to leave my arms. I put her down and she stood tightly clutching my hand and smiling up at me, but she wouldn't walk a step. Vanda said that Ruby seldom came to see her now: 'I called her a bitch or a cow, I can't remember which, but we haven't been friendly since.

I suppose you wouldn't stay and mind Jane while I dash off to the shops and make a telephone call?'

I spent the entire morning playing with Jane because Vanda stayed away for hours. When it began to rain we went into the house and I wandered from room to room with her in my arms. I took her into Vanda's bedroom to change her napkin and saw that the Major had left some of his clothes there, or they may have belonged to Vanda's dead husband and she was using them herself because they were too good to give away. Some lovely silk pyjamas and a camel-hair dressing-gown were thrown over a chair, and I could see that with a little alteration they would do very well for Vanda, or the pyjama jacket could be cut up and turned into a dress for Jane, although the silk was a little heavy for such a young child. Then I had the idea that I would make Jane a dress in the sewing class at school. We usually made presents for our parents which were put away in drawers and never used; a dress was really needed and would be far more interesting to make than handkerchief-sachets and nightdress-cases. I knew that a tape-measure would be the last thing I would find in Vanda's house, so I cut some strips of paper from magazines with nail-scissors and measured Jane with them, allowing for the fact that she might grow while I was sewing the dress. When Vanda returned she came running up the stairs. She seemed a little annoyed when she found us in the bedroom; in future she would prefer it if I stayed downstairs.

Mrs Alexander was dreadfully hurt that I had been absent when Povey called for me. She said she had been so disappointed it had made her ill and her face had swollen in some sinister way. She told me that it often did this when her feelings were hurt and that sometimes her nose would swell into a long trunk. 'How would you like it if you arrived on my doorstep and a large pink trunk came waving through the letter-box?' she added laughingly. I knew she was joking, but it terrified me all the same because I could imagine it so well.

After a meal of pink soup and bananas and honey Povey drove us somewhere miles into the country because Mrs Alexander had heard that bloodhounds were bred there. When we reached a bleak village where they had once made nails, she started inquiring at cottages about bloodhounds. Some of the women who answered the door slammed it in her face, others giggled and one, who was wearing a man's cap back to front, said: 'I don't know, I'm sure. If it's fox terriers you are wanting, old Jack has a couple.'

'No, no, bloodhounds, you fool,' Mrs Alexander said, in an exasperated voice and from somewhere in the cottage an even more exasperated voice snarled: 'Who the hell are you calling a fool?'

As we were leaving the village behind us Mrs Alexander suddenly noticed a farm perched on the top of a hill and immediately decided that must be where the bloodhounds were kept. As we drove up the hill she said she could hear them baying, but the car was making such a noise in bottom gear I couldn't hear anything. It had started to rain, but Povey couldn't stop to put the hood up because both he and the car had considerable difficulty starting on hills, so we drove on. As soon as we reached the farm, Mrs Alexander leapt out of the car, saying she could smell bloodhounds, and rushed towards the house, her high, golden heels sinking into the mud and the hanging fur on the bottom of her coat growing damper and damper.

I followed behind, sniffing a most unpleasant smell. If that was what bloodhounds smelt of, I didn't want to have anything to do with them. Then I saw what was causing it. There was a huge mound of rubbish heaped up in a field at the side of the house – rotting vegetables, broken china, thousands of empty tins (mostly sardine, tomato and salmon), old rags and mattresses, horns – masses of horns – and some hoofs and a mountain of slimy ash and hen's manure. The rubbish dump was as large as the house and, if it had not smelt so revolting, I would have liked to explore it for treasure; some of the broken china looked interesting, particularly the remains of a pink mug with 'Remember me' painted on it and there was a three-legged iron cooking-pot like cannibals use. As I examined the dump, Mrs Alexander was banging a great iron knocker on the front door, but no bloodhounds bayed and there was no sound of bolts being withdrawn. I glanced at the dirty windows and they all looked blind and the door dumb and I knew that no one lived there. It took some time to get Mrs Alexander to believe this and, when she did, she forgot about bloodhounds and started rushing round the house, peering in all the outhouses and saying she was intending to buy it and turn it into a private zoo. I left her talking in Italian to some pigeons she had discovered sheltering in a shed, while I sat and shivered behind Povey, listening to the rain falling on the canvas hood and dodging the raindrops that came through. Eventually Mrs Alexander emerged from the back of the house with her wet turban slightly awry and her golden slipper golden no longer, but she was chattering away about buying the farm and breeding bears and other rare animals for zoos and perhaps using it as a music centre as well. As we returned through the village, people with grim faces peered at us through windows and open doors.

Eleven

THE eleven o'clock break was just ending when a girl with red hair clashing with her mauve face came running into the classroom to tell me that someone had called for me and was waiting in the hall. She had interrupted a discussion on what had happened to Elizabeth Barrett Browning's neck and I was thinking about this as I left the room. Had she never had a neck or was it due to illness or bad posture, I wondered? Then my thoughts were scattered by hearing excited laughter and chattering coming from the classroom and I realized there must be a joke about my visitor. I peered with apprehension into the main hall, not wanting to be made a fool of, but on the other hand not wanting to miss anything. To my dismay I saw a tiny, upright figure with pointed, golden shoes standing on the black and white tiles, looking like a chessman, a violet turban over an ashen face and a thin little body dressed in a tight black and white dress with a slit all up one side. Mrs Alexander had invaded my school.

My first reaction was to return to the classroom, then I realized the best course was to get her out of the building before anyone else saw her. At the same time as she noticed me half-hiding against the wall, the school bell started clanging, causing her to put her hands over her ears and exclaim:

'Must they make that din?' I assured her that masses more bells were due to ring any minute and gently guided her to the front steps, telling her that my English lesson was about to start. It was the first time I had touched her and her arm did not feel like a human arm, more like a thin rag-doll's. When I had steered her safely to the top of the steps, I asked her why she had come. Had she wanted to see me about anything in particular? She fixed her huge, slightly unfocused eyes on me: 'No, dear. I just wanted to see you. I'm lonely, you know.' She placed her thin hand on my shoulder and absent-mindedly pinched it. 'Don't forget that Povey will be calling for you on Saturday. I may have something exciting to show you, something I am expecting by train from London.'

Another bell rang and I said: 'Yes, of course I'll come, but I must leave you now, I'm dreadfully late as it is,' and I ran off to my classroom to face an angry mistress and a considerable amount of teasing.

I tried to pass Mrs Alexander off as a famous pianist, but it didn't work because some of the girls already knew her; one called her the Monkey Queen and another the Mad Mustard Pot. They insisted that she was some relation of mine and even Esmé was teased about her. The thought that she might appear at the school weighed on my mind and made it even harder to concentrate on my lessons.

Saturday turned out to be one of those wet days when it seems as if the rain will never cease, great grey drops falling out of the sky with a horrible regularity. I felt I wasn't missing much when I drove off in the car with Povey and dodged the rain that leaked in through the hood. The little ones had been in a whining mood because Mrs Hand wouldn't allow them to play shops in the kitchen, and Toby had lost the magnet with which he made all the metal handles on the furniture move – we always had to be surprised when he did it. Esmé was cleaning out her mice. She had started with one female, but it had managed to get crossed with a wild mouse and now there were about twenty piebald mice living in the cage. She was seriously thinking of letting them all loose in the Lawrences' stables. She had outgrown mice and I didn't want to take them over because of the smell.

We bounced along the road, stopping every now and again for Povey to buy animal and human food from the queer little shops Mrs Alexander patronized. When we reached the house, I remembered that there was to be a surprise. As we entered the hall the parrot screamed out: 'Antonio, Antonio' as usual and the greyhound with the goitre gave a feeble wave with its long thin tail and delicately sniffed at Povey's parcels. There was something in a box by the fire, but I didn't have time to examine it because Mrs Alexander called me from upstairs.

I found her in the bathroom washing a black fur coat. The bath was stained an extraordinary reddish colour that matched the wispy bits of her hair that crept out from beneath her turban. She was bashing the fur about with violent energy and I asked if it was good for it. 'Good for it? There's nothing better for fur than a good wash. Then hang it out in the rain to dry and the soft water gets right into the skin.' She gave the coat a final bash and asked me to pull the plug out of the bath.\ There was no chain and I didn't like putting my hand into the dirty water, but with her awful eyes fixed on me I had to. Accidentally I touched the coat and it was all slimy and curly, although it was wet. Mrs Alexander called down the stairs for Povey to carry the coat into the garden and, as he lifted it out of the bath, she looked at it with pride and said as if to herself: 'Real astrakhan. I wonder if I could sell it. Astrakhan, the skin of the unborn lamb.' Then, turning to me: 'They tear them from their mothers' wombs, you know.' I went downstairs.

She soon followed me, saying: 'Now for the surprise. Let me show you Beppo, the new monkey. He's larger than the others, rather a common fellow, really.' She went to the box by the fire and extracted a big brown monkey. He was the sort that go with barrel-organs, and he had the saddest face. There was a strap with a chain attached round his waist and Mrs Alexander held one end of the chain while he crouched on the floor, looking pathetic. She asked him in the arch way she used to speak to animals how he liked his new home and mistress and the answer to her question was a bite on the leg. When the screaming was over and Beppo chattering away in his box, Mrs Alexander pulled down her black silk stocking and examined three little holes in her blue-white leg. I had to examine them too and displeased her by saying they resembled the bite I had once received from a mole I tried to capture. At first she said she would burn the wound with a red-hot iron, but eventually she settled on iodine. I had to apply the iodine while she shut her eyes and gave little cries of anguish as if she were being tortured. At last the bite was cleaned and covered with corn plaster, and the black silk stocking, now laddered, was pulled up and safely attached to suspenders. I was glad to be finished with that nauseating white leg.

With an exaggerated limp Mrs Alexander hobbled off to the kitchen to give the unfortunate Povey instructions about luncheon, but when she returned the limp was forgotten and she was carrying two glasses of sherry on a tarnished silver tray. She said we needed it and I certainly felt much happier after I had drunk it. We sat either side of the fire, twisting our empty glasses in our hands, and Mrs Alexander told me about a lover she had once had – an Italian admiral who had followed her to England at a most inconvenient time when she was wandering round a deserted country vicarage with a chamber-pot in her hand. She told me too about her lovely mother standing at the top of a double staircase to receive her guests. All her memories of her mother seemed to be social ones. Every now and again she would become quiet and glare at the monkey's box. In all the years she had kept monkeys she had never been bitten before and she was going to break this one's will.

We ate baked fish swimming in grey gravy and listened to the rain. I was becoming bored and depressed as the effect of the sherry wore off and would have even welcomed helping Mrs Alexander clean the tawdry orange drawing-room or the surgery. I interrupted a story about someone in Russia having their noses rubbed in snow to combat frost-bite and asked if we couldn't boil some instruments. She gave me rather a sly glance and said: 'No, the instruments can wait. I am about to give you a demonstration of animal training which I think you will enjoy. Before the afternoon is over Beppo will be completely subservient to me. Although I intend to treat him with the utmost kindness, I shall break his will.' She rang a little hand-bell for Povey to clear the dirty plates away, but there was no answer – evidently he had gone home for the afternoon. As I helped her take the things into the kitchen I said: 'As a matter of fact I'd prefer not to see you training Beppo, anyway not today. I think the rain has made me a bit tired.' She gave me another of those sly looks as she sipped a second glass of sherry and asked: 'Do you think I shall be unkind to the animal? Surely you know me better than that?' I hastily assured her that, although I knew she would be kind, I felt it wasn't a good day for training animals – so wet and dismal. She put her empty glass on the draining-board and almost snarled: 'What an extraordinary child you are! Surely you don't think I shall take the animal outside and expose it to this filthy climate?'

I dared not say any more and sadly put down the dirty bowls I was holding and followed her into the hall. I was a little reassured when I saw her take a banana from a bowl on the table and walk towards Beppo's box with it. She pushed a piece of banana through one of the air-holes, and a bit later a little hand came out for more. This went on for some time and I forgot my apprehension and became interested to see what she planned to do next. Then she gently opened the lid of the box. Nothing happened for a moment except a strong smell of monkey. Suddenly Beppo shot out with a wild look in his light eyes, leapt on to the chimney-piece and perched there, nervously scratching himself and chattering with his forehead all wrinkled like a man's. Mrs Alexander went towards him with a piece of banana in her hand, but he ignored her and, when she started talking to him in Italian, which she seemed to think was a language all animals understood, he took a flying leap on to the mother-of-pearl table, which tottered and fell on to the tiled floor, scattering thin pieces of pearl. The crash terrified him, but he kept quite still for a moment, just chittering and chatter-ing. Then he leapt at Mrs Alexander with teeth bared, making frightful noises. The next thing I knew was that she was shouting in the most blood-curdling language and Beppo was savagely biting her arms and hands. She implored me to pull him off, but I was far too frightened and made for the front door. By the time I had reached it she had mastered Beppo and was beating him with the poker, her arms and hands bloody and her turban slipping from her cropped head. She yelled at me: 'I forbid you to leave the house, you little coward.' Her face was all distorted and her lips were not there any more. But her head! It was dreadful, all scabs and holes. I ran. The last thing I saw was the awful black coat made of unborn lambs hanging from a tree, dripping in the rain.

I'd left my school coat behind, but I knew I could never return for it. That holey head! It reminded me of an ugly thing an old woman had once given my father, a man's head made of china. He was bald and had an awful laugh on his face and his head was full of holes to contain matches. But the holes in Mrs Alexander's head were far too large for matches, more suitable for candles. When I thought of her with candles burning in her head, I was sick in the road and felt considerably better afterwards.

I never saw Mrs Alexander again. I heard that she gave up her car after being summoned for using it when it was not taxed and the last news I had of her was rather unexpected. She had taken up roller-skating.

Twelve

IT WAS A RELIEF when the summer term ended and I
could look forward to seven weeks' freedom. The girls had
ceased to tease me about my supposed relation, Mrs
Alexander; it was now the Holy Ghost. During a scripture
class I had been rash enough to say that I liked the Holy
Ghost the best of the Trinity because he seemed so lonely.
The idea had just struck me and the words were out before
I could stop them. The mistress who was taking the class
told me that I was irreligious because one did not 'like' the
Holy Trinity, one worshipped them. Some of the girls were
laughing behind the upraised lids of their desks as they pretended to fumble for pencils and others gave me incredulous
or reproachful glances, and of course they all set on me as
soon as the lesson came to an end. I only had to stand the
teasing for a few days before we broke up. Next term my
remark would be forgotten and many of us would have
moved to another form. I myself shouldn't, because I was
only managing to hang on to my present one by the skin of
my teeth and Esmé's help. I wondered if the school staff
noticed the difference between my homework and the work
I did in class.

Polly was spending the holidays in Switzerland and John

had been invited to a school friend's home in Devonshire for the latter half of August, so we were to be a small family. Walking home from school the last day, Esmé and I agreed that perhaps it was just as well, because the family finances were in a shaky state. One afternoon a man wearing a mackintosh had actually delivered a summons. Mother had taken it calmly, but we were filled with foreboding, although she assured us that a summons was nothing, just another form of bill; her father's house had been filled with them when she was a girl and they had even had the bailiffs once. Mother's father had been the brother of Uncle Lawrence, but he seemed to have been a very different sort of man. He had the same passion for horses, but it had taken the form of race-horses and he had died in early middle age, a ruined man.

When we returned home on that last day of term, we found Mother in the middle of selling the piano to an elderly man in a rat-coloured suit, who said his wife had always wanted a piano. 'I saw your advert in the local paper, see,' he was saying in a deep oily voice. 'I said to Mother: "Why, there's a piano for sale that might suit you down to the ground" – so here I am. Could one of you young ladies tickle the ivories to give me an idea as to tone? Mother can't play herself, see, but she does like a piano with tone.' He beamed on us both and we beamed back. Esmé sat down and played 'The Blue Danube', which gave him great pleasure and convinced him that the 'piana' had real tone. He gave Mother twelve pounds for it, including the stool, more than enough to clear our main debts. Now there only remained the problem of keeping the Lawrences out of the drawing-room so that they would not notice the piano was missing and ask questions. 'It's not that I have done anything wrong,' Mother explained rather pathetically, 'it's just that they wouldn't understand how difficult it is to manage on such a small income. I think the cost of living must have gone up recently.'

When John came home, he was restless and I could tell he was longing to join his friend in Devonshire. They had planned to do a lot of sailing and John was wildly excited about it. He had bought a book on the subject and read it over and over again, often quoting from it out loud to us and showing us how to tie knots and distinguish between sloops, cutters, yawls, etc., from small black and white illustrations. Secretly I was bored with tying knots, but I copied some of the boat pictures on a large scale and John pinned them on his bedroom walls, which pleased me very much.

The day before John left for Devonshire was one of those sultry, threatening days, glaring white with the sun staring behind the clouds. In spite of the heat, the family had planned to have a picnic on the banks of the canal, but my head ached and I did not feel like taking such a long walk. Also I wanted to take Jane the dress I had made for her in the school sewing class. I had sat up late the previous evening finishing it – which perhaps accounted for the headache – and now it was finished I couldn't wait another day to see how it looked on her. It was made of blue shantung, rather shiny. I'd embroidered daisies on the bodice and there were pink French knots round the neck and hem. I was extremely proud of it because it was the first piece of clothing for human wearing I'd made. I did have a few regrets about missing the picnic when I saw Mother and Esmé cutting sandwiches, three different kinds, into little squares, and, besides the tea in thermos-flasks, ginger beer. It was the kind with glass balls like marbles stuck on top. You pressed the ball in against a fence or anything handy and drank from the bottle and there was the terrifying but exciting thought that your tongue might get sucked into the bottle. We were told by other children that this quite frequently happened, although we had never met anyone it had happened to or seen children being taken to the doctor with bottles hanging from their tongues.

I stood at the dining-room window, regretfully watching them leave The Hollies carrying the square sandwiches, the glass-stoppered pop and the thermos in two withy baskets. I had just noticed there was a bag of Chelsea buns, the ones that unwrap into a long piece of dough. John carried two home-made fishing-rods and Esmé the baskets; she said she preferred to carry two because they balanced. Toby was carrying a fishing-net and jam-jar and Clare a bottle containing milk, which she shook from time to time – she had discovered that you could make butter that way. Mother went to rest upstairs and the house seemed lonely after they had gone. It was more noticeable, the kind of house it was, when it was quiet or empty. Things like the encrusted paper half-way up the hall walls hit you in the eye, and the hideous tiled floor and the squares of stained glass set high in the dining-room window. There was a slightly mean smell as well. I listlessly hunted for tissue paper and found some in the broom cupboard under the stairs, which smelt of paraffin. I carefully wrapped Jane's dress, tied the parcel with blue ribbon taken from Mother's night-dress and left the depressing house.

I was feeling extremely hot when I reached Vanda's and took a short cut through the farmyard which I usually avoided after I had seen men doing something awful to young pigs. It was almost deserted, just a kindly Rhode Island hen with a family of white chickens following her and a man mixing bran-mash in a huge iron pot. I opened the kitchen door and called to Vanda and, as there was no reply, I went to the foot of the stairs and called again. This time her voice came floating down to me, so I followed it upstairs. I found her sitting on the bedroom floor, surrounded by what appeared to be the entire contents of her wardrobe. She glanced up for a moment, then smiled ruefully as she said: 'I'm just going through my things, darling: did you ever see such rags? Far too bad to mend, I should say, but of course I can't sew, so what's the use?' She tossed a pink *crêpe de Chine* petticoat into the air. 'Perhaps if I wrote to Mother she would send me a few things. She is as mean as hell usually, but she wouldn't like to think of me wearing no underclothes, shock her to the core most likely.'

'Yes,' I agreed, 'people do take underclothes seriously. There was a woman called Dulcie Bennet in our village, a sloppy-looking woman, who everyone said wore no under-clothes. The boys used to sing after her as she passed down the street: "Nobody knows, nobody knows whether she's got any underclothes." It would be awful if they sung that after you.'

Vanda stood up and kicked the clothes into a heap. 'You do say the most idiotic things sometimes,' she exclaimed crossly. Then, brightening: 'What's in that intriguing little parcel?'

Although I told her it was a surprise present for Jane, she insisted on opening it, tearing at the tissue paper with her long thin fingers and dropping the blue ribbon on the floor. I couldn't help being pleased when she praised my sewing, but she disconcerted me by adding: 'Perhaps you could help me with some of these things,' nodding towards the bundle on the floor. 'I'd no idea you could sew so well.'

We went into the room where Jane slept among the trunks. She had a proper cot, but the bottom was always falling out, although I had mended it several times with string. Jane was standing up and holding on to the bars of the cot, looking disconsolate. She smiled when she saw me and held up her arms to be lifted out. As I held her close to me I was surprised that she felt so light, almost like a dry, dead bird, but she was happy enough when I put her down, and walked beside me, holding my hand, looking up, beaming with pride, and sometimes letting go of my hand and taking a few stamping steps alone, that ended with a run and a fall. I washed her and put on the new dress, which fitted her perfectly. Then I brushed her long hair and tied it into a little knob with the blue ribbon. When I showed her her reflection in the looking-glass, she was not interested. What she really enjoyed was the feel of the silky material. She kept stroking it and smiling. Vanda said she looked almost pretty and I must make her more clothes as soon as possible.

We had tea on the long dry grass in the garden and drank out of mugs because all the cups were broken. We ate bread and butter with brown sugar sprinkled on it, very crunchy and sweet – I've never eaten brown sugar since, although I can still taste it in my imagination.

The sky remained a glaring white, very still except for the constant humming of insects and the occasional rumble of carts passing down the lane. I carefully broke up small pieces of bread and butter for Jane, because I didn't want her to feed herself and make her dress sticky, and she kept opening her mouth like a baby bird and saying: 'More' – it was one of the few words she knew.

When we had finished our tea Vanda said: 'Do you think you could face that pile of underclothes? If you'd sew on a few shoulder-straps it would be something.' So we collected the mugs and tea-pot and went into the dark house, Jane stumbling after us. She was crazy about walking now and even wanted to climb the stairs. We sat on the floor of Vanda's big bedroom with the door and window open because of the heat. It was really a beautiful room, with a beamed ceiling and whitewashed walls. There was little furniture in it, and what there was was maid's bedroom stuff except for the bow-fronted dressing-table with its triple mirror and white woodwork, decorated with hand-painted flowers. Vanda said it had been one of her twenty-first birth-day presents, just before she was married. There was a photo-graph of her dead husband in a silver frame on one side of the dressing-table and a leather-framed one of her mother in an old-fashioned presentation dress, looking soulful under her crest of feathers. Vanda sat smoking while I sewed on shoulder-straps with a rusty needle. I said I'd bring my sew-ing-basket another time. The only scissors she had were tiny, meant for embroidery and shaped like a stork. You cut with the beak, only this stork had a blunt beak. Jane stumped round the room with a petticoat over her head, lifting it from time to time to peer at us and laugh. Vanda looked at her through her cigarette-smoke and said wanly: 'She was difficult enough to manage when she lay in her pram all day, but this walking is the limit. You have to watch her all the time.' As I struggled to get the rusty needle through the silk I suddenly felt depressed and wished I was home. My head was aching sharply at the back and I imagined a golden saw was sawing it in two. I handed Vanda the night-gown I had been cobbling together and said: 'Vanda, I'll have to go home. My head's aching and I can't see properly. I'll come back and finish these things another day, really I will.'

Looking almost like Aunt Lawrence, she said primly that I was too young to have headaches. Then suddenly her face lit up and all resemblance to Aunt Lawrence vanished. She sprang from the floor and ran to the open door. 'Listen,' she cried, 'isn't that Dick's car?' and, turning her glowing face towards me: 'All right, darling, leave the mending if you want to, but take Jane for a walk in the pram. It will do your headache good – it will be good for both of you.'

She looked away again, listening to the roar of the Major's powerful car as it turned into the lane, then she rushed to-wards the head of the stairs. I shouted after her: 'Look out!

Jane's disappeared,' but I doubt if she heard. I threw down the sewing and hurried after her. I could see her running down the landing rather awkwardly in her narrow-skirted green dress, one hand held out towards the banisters and the other adjusting her sleek black hair. I can still see her running like that in her daffodil-leaf dress, her high heels stamping in the brown oilcloth decorated with yellow swastikas, and the picture at the end of the landing of a woman shielding a candle with one hand and the light glowing through. And I can still see a small pink and blue figure stumping along at the head of the stairs looking like a mobile heap of clothes. Suddenly it was not there any more, there was only Vanda holding on to the banisters screaming and holding her throat as if to stop the screams. She was all doubled up and her eyes were closed, but when she opened them she turned away from the stairs and looked at me with unseeing eyes. I slowly walked towards her and looked down the staircase and saw what I knew I would see. Jane was lying sideways on the stone floor and the pink petticoat was lying half-way down the dirty stairs. Vanda had ceased to scream and was saying brokenly: 'I didn't see her. I didn't know she was there.' She ran down and went as if to take Jane in her arms, but drew back. I thought 'You fool! Hold her, love her, do something to make her warm,' but she did nothing at all. As I went down to join her, I saw the Major coming out of the afternoon shadows. 'What's going on? What are you doing?' he demanded petulantly. Then he saw Jane lying on the stones looking like a wax doll and he muttered: 'She's only stunned. Pick her up, can't you, and wrap her in a blanket! Don't stand there like a couple of ninnies. Look, I'll fetch a doctor if you like.'

Vanda staggered towards him. 'No, no, don't leave me. I think she's . . .' She swayed and would have fallen if he had not helped her to a chair. He held her head down low.

I did not know why at the time and thought he was doing it to be unkind. I picked Jane up. Perhaps it would have been better if I had left her where she was, because her head lolled on one side and a trickle of blood came from her mouth. She had become extraordinarily heavy in a very short time, no longer like a dry, dead bird. I said: 'She's leaking,' but no one listened.

The Major, crimson in the face, was holding Vanda's head down and her black hair was touching the floor. I felt afraid of them as if they were doing something evil, and crept upstairs with Jane and laid her on Vanda's bed, wiping her mouth on the sheet. No more blood came, but her eyes had gone white and, although she felt warm, I was sure she was dead. I lay on the bed beside her and tried to breathe life into her mouth, which was slightly open.

After a time they came into the room, Vanda and the Major, and I turned away from their faces. Vanda asked in a shaking voice: 'Is she conscious yet?' No one answered. She bent down over us and saw the white eyes without pupils, drew back and cried: 'The eyes, my God, the eyes!' Then she attacked me, hitting my face and shouting in a terrible blurred voice: 'You did it, you killed my baby. I saw you knock her down the stairs.' I tried to get away from her hard hands and struggled to take refuge under the bed and was almost underneath when the Major dragged her away and smacked her face, telling her to stop behaving like a bloody fool. He said Jane was to be taken to hospital immediately and, snatching a blanket from the bed, pushed it at Vanda. 'Wrap the child in that, and for Christ's sake pull yourself together before we reach the hospital,' he bellowed.

Then he bent down as if to pick up Jane, but recoiled and stood over Vanda while she did it with her face averted. She was mumbling: 'I know she's dead. It isn't my fault, it's her fault; she was supposed to be looking after Jane.' They slowly left the room together, but as I was crawling from under the bed the Major returned to say: 'As for you, leave this house immediately, and if you don't keep your chattering little mouth shut, you'll find yourself in trouble, great trouble.' He clapped his hands together sharply and shouted: 'Scram', then left the room.

I dared not 'scram' past him, so waited under the bed until I heard the car start. When I heard the engine throbbing I crept out and left the farm for the last time. I don't remember walking out of it, I just found myself standing in the lane.

The extraordinary thing was that I couldn't remember the way home either. Somehow I managed to reach the road. The white dust was so deep, it seemed to prevent my legs moving properly and the tall cow-parsley on the sides of the road was doing a horrible dance, now beckoning, now re-treating. It was difficult to breathe; I thought that perhaps the dust had become so deep I was filling up with it. I became surrounded by it and above a great roar I heard my voice crying: 'I'm drowning, I'm drowning in dust.' I remember an enormous man, dressed in white like a cricketer, lifting me from the road and saying from a long distance that I was a little fool and had almost been run over. 'What were you doing walking in the middle of the road? Didn't you hear my horn?' he was demanding, and the question echoed round my head. Then he added in a kinder tone: 'You're all right, aren't you? I didn't hit you?' I answered: 'No, it was someone else that hit me. She said I'd killed her baby, but I saw her send it flying down the stairs. She was running to meet the Major when she did it.'

The huge white man stood there bewilderedly biting the big moustache he hid behind. He helped me into his car, then entered by the other door and sat beside me, a great white mountain of a man. I looked at him carefully and said: 'I know you. You're the brass-founder.' He smiled and said: 'That's true, but I'm afraid I don't know who you are or where you live. Just tell me and I'll drive you straight home.' It was his speaking so kindly that made it worse, and I had to admit that I didn't quite know where I did live, and it was difficult to say even that because I was crying so much. I don't remember what happened after that, except that he got me home and Mother kept saying: 'Concussion', and feeling my head with her cool hand and I wished she wouldn't.

Later, a doctor I had never seen before was talking about shock and brain fever. I don't know how long I stayed in bed, perhaps a week or two. Sometimes I knew where I was and could feel the sheets, but when I opened my eyes there was a horrible light as if the room was on fire. Afterwards I discovered they had hung a red blind over the window. Most of the time I was in a frightening dream that kept coming and going in waves. It was as if I were feeling things with the ends of my fingers, rough and smooth things, and this roughness and smoothness seemed to be enveloping me. Sometimes I thought I could see a picture of two ugly women resembling parrots and wearing large old-fashioned hats. Out of one's mouth came a balloon with the words: 'See thora' written inside. Then a morning came when I knew what was causing the red light and made out the chest of drawers which was right against my bed and I could feel the painted white wood properly with my fingers, no longer rough and smooth. I thought it must be Christmas because there was a heap of parcels on top of the chest of drawers, but I had no desire to open them. Some time later I discovered my hair had gone. I was not bald, but it had been cut almost as short as a boy's. I knew people were always coming into my room – I'd vaguely seen them in a red mist – but now they were real people. One was a nurse

148

who said she was called Nurse Fenner, and whose belt creaked when she breathed. Mother was flitting in and out, wearing a mauve dress I'd never seen before. I heard her tell the nurse that it was made of voile and washed like a rag. Esmé put her head round the door and grinned shyly and vanished. I noticed that her bed had been taken from my room.

During the night rough and smooth came back, but every day I felt more awake. The red blind was pulled up and Esmé came in and asked if I would like to know what was in the parcels. It pleased me to think of them piled up and unopened, it was something real to look forward to, but I could tell she was dying to open them to see my reactions, so I nodded. Talking was still an awful effort. She took my scissors from the sewing-box and started to cut the string; there was a rustling of paper and she produced an open box containing little paper tents of many colours. It was a sort of game of hoop-la in which the paper caps had to be somersaulted into holes cut in cardboard. The colours of the paper tents were pale and charming, and when I put one on each finger it was as if they were wearing dunces' caps. There was a box of different metal puzzles – the thought of struggling with them made me feel tired and I pushed them away – and a *Girl's Own Annual*: I was pleased about this because it was a promotion from *Little Folks* and read by girls much older than I was – Polly had only recently given it up. The last parcel of all was square and I could see it was heavy by the way Esmé held it. She said: 'This is the best present of all, so I think you had better open it yourself,' and she laid it down on the bed and cut the string. I managed to sit up and clumsily unwrapped the paper and exposed a toffee-coloured leather writing-case, embossed with my initials, with a lock and two keys and the most fascinating pen I had ever seen. It was made of hollow glass filled with light green liquid and a little white shell was inside. In some mysterious way when I held the pen upside down, the shell became caught in an air bubble for a few seconds.

They told me that the writing-case was a present from the brass-founder and that he had become a frequent visitor to the house. He had a name now – Mr Blackwell – and, as I lay in bed, I sometimes heard his big car purring outside the house.

I tried not to think about Vanda and the baby and, when they came pushing into my mind too much, I pretended to myself that it was only an ill dream. But all the time I knew it was true.

One morning when Mother stood by my bed looking down at me, I said: 'It's true about Jane, isn't it?' For a moment she appeared startled, then she tucked up the bedclothes that did not need tucking and said, with her face down: 'I don't know what you mean, darling. I think I did hear something about them leaving the village, but I really don't know for certain.' She left the clothes alone and added brightly: 'Do you know, that extraordinary woman, Mrs Alexander, turned up while you were ill? She was all dressed as a nurse – it looked very strange with the gold shoes – and wanted to nurse you, but fortunately I was able to tell her we already had a nurse. Even then it was difficult to get rid of her. I must say she's the last person one would want around when there's illness in the house.'

For the moment I forgot about Jane and sat up in bed and cried: 'You won't let her in if she comes again? Please don't let her in.'

The first day I was allowed downstairs for an hour or two the nurse left. I was almost well again and could do things for myself. Rough and smooth had gone away and I could read without getting a headache. My cropped hair had turned into a crown of curls and was easy to manage. I secretly hoped I looked like Nell Gwyn, although Esmé called me Golly. I liked her calling me Golly because, when I first came downstairs, the family were almost shy of me and I was made to feel like a visitor. Even Aunt Lawrence talked to me in a false, bright way, although she meant to be kind and brought butter, cream and eggs in little baskets and once took me for a drive in the dog-cart.

After a few days Esmé's bed was brought back to our room. Now I would ask her about Jane and all the other things that were weighing on my mind. Had the Lawrences found out about the piano? Who had paid for the nurse and were we dreadfully short of money? I lay in my black iron bed, waiting for Esmé to join me, and studied the familiar damp marks on the ceiling. One was almost a policeman wearing a helmet and another a three-legged dog and there was quite a good map of Ireland over Esmé's bed. It was almost dark when she entered the room, carrying a candle, shielding its light with her hand exactly as the woman in the picture did. The glowing red hand terrified me and I sat up in bed and shouted: 'Take your hand away from the candle, I can't bear it.' Esmé said reassuringly: 'It's nothing. I didn't want to disturb you with the light.' She placed the candle on the chest of drawers and told me to go to sleep. I stayed humped up in bed and said I couldn't go to sleep until she told me about Jane. 'She's dead, I know she is. Blood was coming out of her mouth and her eyes had gone all horrible. You know, Vanda ran into her at the top of the stairs and then she tried to say I'd done it. Oh, Esmé, she was so happy that day, stumping about and laughing, and it ended so quickly.'

I would have rambled on, but Esmé stopped me. 'But she isn't dead. Surely you knew that? Jane is in hospital all packed up in plaster, but she's alive. It was all in the local paper. It may still be in the broom cupboard and you can read it for yourself tomorrow. It said something about Vanda seeing her heading for the stairs and trying to catch her but being a moment too late. It didn't say it was her fault, although everyone in the village is saying it was, because she didn't have a gate put up. I think she has left the farm for good, but no one knows where she has gone.'

The wonderful relief that Esmé's words brought! I lay in bed, completely happy and relaxed. The fact that Jane was seriously injured in hospital meant little to me then; all I cared about was that she was still alive, that her mother had not killed her and that the dreadful white eyes were only a thing of the moment and that one day she would be laughing and stumping about again.

Thirteen

MR BLACKWELL, the brass-founder, became a frequent visitor to our house. He was a shy man, hiding behind his drooping Arabian Nights moustache, and at first his visits only lasted a few minutes. He would gravely ask how we all were and if there was anything he could do. Usually when he had gone we would discover a basket of peaches had been left on the hall bench or a wooden box of Turkish delight; once it was half a dozen honeycombs. We never saw him bring anything into the house, but when he had gone we found these lovely things. We soon learnt not to thank him because he would back away in horror if we did, once even falling down our front steps in an effort to escape our gratitude.

It was John who discovered he was crazy about aeroplanes and knew how to fly them. He had been up in a gas balloon when he was a young man, and I could imagine him sitting like an enormous hen in a tiny nest, sailing through the skies. But it was aeroplanes he loved and quite soon he was showing us the models he had made. He was too diffident to bring them into the house unless we asked to see them; then he would mumble that perhaps there was one in the back of the car and would amble out and return with an elaborate model. We would follow him out to a near-by field and watch a demonstration, which frequently resulted in the aeroplane crashing and becoming hopelessly broken, an occurrence which distressed us more than it did him. John could talk reasonably intelligently about aeroplanes – I suppose he had picked it up from boys at school – but the rest of the family knew hardly anything about them. We occasionally saw one flying over the village, but, except for the sound of their engine, they could have been crows.

On the last day of John's holidays Mr Blackwell asked the whole family for luncheon at his house. Remembering what happened on my last visit, I was a little afraid of entering the house again, but the rest of us were delighted with the invitation. We had heard from Mrs Hand about the glittering white paint and the three bathrooms, the electric light made by an engine in the yard, the carpets with pile as deep as hay, and three great red dogs with bald tails.

The red dogs with the bald tails were the first thing we met as we walked up the well-kept drive. They were the colour of raw liver and, except for their tails, were covered in negro-like curls. Although they barked a lot, they were the most friendly things and leapt and squirmed round us, panting and wagging their poor tails and showing the whites of their eyes. Mother said they were Irish water spaniels and very rare, she had not seen one for years.

Mr Blackwell must have heard the dogs' greeting because he came out of the house to welcome us. He was wearing a long jacketed suit decorated with large black and white checks – you could almost have played draughts on it. Although Mother and John flinched, I liked it. Toby must have too, because he ran up to him and, hugging one of his stork-like legs, said: 'You are the biggest man I've ever seen, good enough to be a giant.' We all stood outside the house for a few minutes and Mother complimented him on its appearance: 'I've known this house since I was a child, but I can't remember ever seeing it newly painted before. It must have been painted sometimes, but it was always flaking off when I saw it. I'm glad you've kept it white.' She looked nervously around, in case he had vulgarized the place. 'I see you have had the old mud walls repaired, I'm glad of that. And the stables, are they still the same? There used to be an old clock tower, I remember, and a loft with a flight of stone steps leading up to it. I used to play here as a child when I stayed with my grandparents at Tower Hill, but I can't remember coming to Springfield after I grew up.'

Mr Blackwell assured her that the stables were untouched and that he had even left the same names on the loose-box doors, adding apologetically: 'I only keep one horse and, to tell the truth, I'm terrified of it and find it a little hard learning to ride at my time of life; I'd far rather fly a plane, but I'm persevering. You see, I had ideas about hunting and all that sort of thing when I bought the house, but I realize now I'm not a country man. I'm a machine man, mad about speed.'

He suddenly became embarrassed and hustled us into the house. A maid took us upstairs to leave our hats and gloves in a bedroom with a huge, puffy pink eiderdown on the bed; and, although the carpets were not quite as deep as hay, they were deep enough, rather like walking on soft snow. Clare took a flying jump, landing in the middle of the eiderdown, and said it was heavenly, like lying in the middle of a cloud; but Mother quickly pulled her off, carefully arranging it as it had been before.

We trailed downstairs and found John and Mr Blackwell drinking sherry in a formal gold and white drawing-room that looked as if it had never been sat in before. We all had a glass of sherry, except the little ones. We sat stiffly on our stiff little chairs until the sherry began to work, then the children noticed the electric light switches and turned the lights on and off, illuminating a beautiful crystal chandelier that had been adapted for electricity, the sort of light the Snow Queen might have had, so icy and glittering. As Esmé leant forward, vaguely listening to Mother and Mr Blackwell discussing the tyranny of gardeners, I noticed a strange lump coming out of her back. For a moment I thought she was becoming deformed, then I saw a piece of white showing below her red pullover. I tentatively gave it a little pull and a lot more white appeared. Esmé turned round to ask: 'What on earth are you doing to my back?' I pulled a little harder and a night-gown appeared. Mother exclaimed sharply: 'Really, Frances, you should have left your night-gown at home!' She was quite annoyed with me, but Esmé was unperturbed and said it must have got caught up in her pullover when she was dressing.

After a lavish luncheon served in a dining-room furnished in massive oak, Mr Blackwell showed us over the house. He explained that the only rooms he had had anything to do with were his office and an outside workroom; the rest of the house had been furnished by a London firm, with the exception of a few odd pieces he had bought with the house – 'Just rubbish except for the stuff they put in the library,' he said, as he opened the library door and revealed a grey and white room with heavy wine-coloured curtains held back from the windows with thick white cords. The books were all in leather-bound sets chosen by the house-furnishers, and neatly arranged on the long oak table were magazines – the *Tatler*, *Bystander*, *Horse and Hound* and *Punch* – as in a dentist's waiting-room. As I looked round the grand and sombre room, I remembered it was the room where I'd eaten chocolates with the General's wife from a round box, the sun streaming in through the filthy windows and the General's wife with black stuff round her eyes and the exotic smell of her scent. Now there was just a faint smell of leather combined with furniture polish, and something a little sad. I thought: 'Surely that is the table that used to be in the grass hall?' Then I looked closely at the chairs and cried: 'The skinny chairs!' Esmé put her hand over her mouth and shouted through it: 'Oh, the skinny chairs!' and then burst into laughter.

Mother said: 'Hush, dears, one should always be quiet in a library,' but John eagerly leant forward to examine the chairs, tapping the leather with his knuckles and making a drumming sound. 'Not the chairs you told me about, Esmé, not the chairs covered with human skin? Oh, sir, did you buy these with the house?'

Mr Blackwell answered rather huffily: 'Yes, yes, I was just telling you. The furniture in here is the only furniture they could use. The rest was burnt or put up in the attics. Camp-beds and kitchen tables, you know.'

I did not stay to hear any more because I wanted to get away from those terrible chairs. The door of the little room we had seen the General's head protruding from was open. I managed to bring myself to glance inside and saw that it had been turned into an office with a business-like desk and photographs of factories on the walls. It looked harmless enough, but I fancied there was a stain under the shining lino, left by the dying General.

As they came from the library Mr Blackwell was saying: 'Extraordinary, really extraordinary. I must get someone to have a look at them.' He opened a side door that led into the garden and we walked out into the autumn sun on well-swept paths, while giant dahlias and chrysanthemums nodded at us from weedless flower-beds. We inspected the newly-made hard tennis-court, where no one played tennis, and the rose garden, where late roses bloomed for the gardener's pleasure, and the stables, which contained only one chestnut horse with white socks and a star on his forehead.

Mr Blackwell gingerly patted him on the neck, wiped his hand on his handkerchief and said he thought he would get used to him in due course. The groom and stable-boy stumbled sleepily down from the loft, wisps of hay sticking to their clothes as they aimlessly tried to appear busy. John asked if we could see the work-room. Mr Blackwell asked incredulously: 'Would you really like to see it? It's just a simple workshop I converted from the old laundry.' He looked at us inquiringly and we all assured him that we were longing to see it and followed him across the yard to an unpainted oak door that had gone a most lovely silver colour from years of sun and rain. 'I wouldn't let them touch this,' he said as he ran his hand over the wood lovingly and opened the door with a large iron key he took from a ledge. We entered a long whitewashed room with blue-prints pinned on the walls, fitted with work-benches littered with tools of every description, glue-pots, rolls of linen and pieces of wood. There were more tools hanging from the walls and aeroplanes suspended from fine wires from the ceiling, masses of them. John was so excited that he stuttered as he showered Mr Blackwell with questions.

Mother looked round with interest and exclaimed: 'How well I remember this room when it was filled with orphans!'

Clare looked worried. 'But why did they keep orphans here? Didn't they let them out?'

Mother said: 'Oh, yes; they were allowed out on Sundays. I used to see them in church, dressed in print frocks with scarlet shawls in winter. I believe they were well looked after in the Lucies' time. They were such a large family and must have used a great deal of linen.'

While Mother reminisced about orphan laundry-maids, Toby discovered the delights of red paint, which he was happily smearing on to a piece of wood with his hands. As we cleaned him with a piece of linen intended for an aeroplane's wing, Mother said: 'Poor child, he's never been allowed to play with paint before,' as if it was another of the trials of being poor. Mr Blackwell and John were so engrossed in aeroplanes that they failed to notice Toby's yells at being parted from his first pot of paint, and as we left the work-room I heard Mr Blackwell say boyishly: 'Do you know, I'd like to chuck brass and really go in for aeroplanes. Imagine seeing my own planes, hundreds of them, zooming overhead.' As he spoke, he and John gazed up at the laundry ceiling as if expecting to see them circling round.

We took Toby, still faintly whimpering, into the house, and by the time we had finished cleaning him on the fluffy white towel in the downstairs bathroom, it did not look the same, although we carefully turned the red parts on the inner side of the rail. It wasn't a real bathroom, just a gentleman's wash-place, but it appeared wonderfully luxurious to us with its pale green tiled walls, glass shelves and white enamel cupboards. There was a row of highly polished brass jugs embossed with large E.B.s, and a great looking-glass completely covering one wall. We had never seen so much of ourselves before, except in distorting mirrors at fairs. It reflected the three of us at once and I noticed with relief that I had grown, the crown of my head actually reached Esmé's eyebrows. It must have started while I'd been ill. I saw below my pink-striped dress a pair of knees no longer round, they could have belonged to a stranger they were so thin and knobby, and my legs had become horse-like with slim ankles. I certainly was not stumpy any more.

Later in the afternoon, Mr Blackwell drove us home in his open car. Mother resolutely held on to her cartwheel hat, lamenting that she had not brought a motoring veil with her, but we took off ours and let the wind blow through our hair so that it appeared that we were travelling even faster than we were. As Mr Blackwell abruptly drove away so that we could not thank him for our interesting day, Mother said sadly: 'I'm sorry for that man returning to an empty, unhappy house. It is a thousand pities he ever bought it, but I suppose it is no worse than living in an hotel as he has been doing for the last few years since his wife's death. All those dogs! I wonder if he can shoot. And the horse he can't ride, the unused tennis-court. Imagine eating meals alone in that huge dining-room day after day.'

The car disappeared, she turned reluctantly to unlock the front door of The Hollies and we clattered into the narrow hall. 'Goodness, how poky it is!' Mother exclaimed. 'I always forget and it's such a shock to return to.' Toby created a diversion by bursting into tears, producing a large brown stone from his trouser pocket and wailing: 'My stone, my lovely stone that smells of cowboy suits. I wanted to give it to that man.' Mother patted his head and said ruefully: 'Poor child, he isn't used to drinking sherry.'

When the new term at the high school commenced, Clare went instead of me because the doctor said I was to 'run wild' for a few months. To prevent me from becoming too wild it had been arranged that I was to take drawing and painting lessons from Miss Scrimpture, the school art mistress. She lived with her aged mother in a small gravy-smelling villa on the edge of the town, and I had to go there two afternoons a week. She had turned the room which should have been a dining-room into a sort of studio and had hung her muddy still-life paintings on the walls. She was mad on poker-work, and for the first week or so I did nothing else. There was an attractive smell of burning wood combined with methylated spirits, and I remember having to squeeze a rubber ball with one hand, which caused the little poker to glow. I burnt swimming fish on a teapot-stand and flower designs into several wooden boxes, and there was a magnificent blotter with a heavy wood cover which I decorated with acorns and pomegranates – some of the pomegranates were halved so that I could burn in every single seed. The poker-work had to stop because Mother found all these boxes and things were becoming a drain on her income and it was decided it would be more economical for me to draw from plaster casts and paint wild flowers in water-colour and make little raffia baskets suitable for Easter eggs.

Mother said it would be a good idea to give the poker-worked blotter to Aunt Lawrence, and looked quite relieved when she saw me leave the house with it under my arm. There was already a feeling of winter in the air and, as I walked up the Straight Mile, yellow sycamore leaves floated past like lonely hands. When I reached Tower Hill I went under the arch into the yard in the hope of seeing my cousin Charles, who had been very kind to me while I had been ill, telling me about his journey to New York in a Dutch boat and interesting things that had happened to him while he had been abroad and reading to me from books he had enjoyed when he had been my age, *Martin Rattler* and *The Gorilla Hunters*. They were not at all the sort of stories I would have read myself, but I enjoyed them, partly because he had such a pleasing voice, deep and gentle. There was no Charles in the yard, but I was astonished to see a handsome young chauffeur I had never seen before, polishing the car and singing to himself between his teeth. A groom, riding one horse and leading another, clattered past and I could see Uncle Lawrence under his brown bowler hat bearing down on me, so I slipped through the green gate that led to the garden. I found Aunt Lawrence and Ruby in the bird-room poring over a copy of the *Daily Mail*. Aunt Lawrence's half smile was there. She looked up and said: 'Good morning, Frances,' and then went on to Ruby: 'I always said that man was a bounder.'

Ruby nodded her narrow head and said with conviction: 'I know for a fact that he made Vanda very unhappy at times. What that girl must be feeling now! I'm sure she was out to marry him.'

I glanced at the newspaper and was startled to see the Major scowling at me, grey and ghost-like. Aunt Lawrence commented: 'Well, he will have to marry this one if the divorce goes through, although I wouldn't put it past him to do a bolt. Still, an earl's daughter, even an immoral one, is better than that disreputable Vanda.'

Ruby held the newspaper close to her near-sighted eyes. 'But she's five years older than the Major, Mother, and look at her dreadful teeth hanging out as if to dry.'

Aunt Lawrence snatched the newspaper back. 'I wish you wouldn't use expressions like that, Ruby. Hum, I see what you mean about the teeth, most unfortunate.'

The room had the sickly smell of caged birds and spiteful women and I stood with my weight first on one leg then on the other, hoping they would ask me to sit down, but they went on grabbing the paper from one another. 'The husband and the gardener actually climbed a ladder and entered the bedroom through the window,' Aunt Lawrence was saying. 'Really, imagine dragging the gardener into it. I suppose the fool was afraid to go up alone.' And then Ruby's plaintive voice: 'And she's the mother of three children, poor little things.'

The birds pecked their seeds and the women their newspaper and no one noticed me standing with my blotter decorated with pomegranates. I silently laid it on the table and left them to their pecking and went out by the garden door. The garden was looking as ugly as ever, with its grey brick paths and box hedges. There were a few chrysanthemums peering over the top, but they were almost the colour of bees and looked as if they had never been young.

The blotter was discovered after I had left and resulted in Aunt Lawrence and Ruby arriving unexpectedly for tea and being surprised at the enormous amount of bread and butter we ate. Mother, seeing them coming in through the gate, snatched the large blue enamel teapot from the table and ran to the kitchen with it, holding it away from her as if it was about to explode. She returned a few minutes later with a shining silver one and a few stale biscuits on a cake-stand. We went on stolidly eating our bread and butter, thickly spread with Mr Blackwell's honey, while Aunt Lawrence thanked me for the blotter and said it was exactly what she needed, but I had noticed that grown-ups always said that before they put the presents that children make away in drawers and forgot about them. Besides the news that Vanda's Major had been involved in a sensational divorce case, there was the new chauffeur to discuss. The old one, who had originally been coachman, was having an operation for gall-stones and felt he would never be up to driving 'that great lummoxing car' again, so he had been pensioned off. 'He's only sixty-six and may live for years,' Aunt Lawrence said regretfully. 'I wonder if I could turn him into a butler, or would that upset the indoor staff? I don't care to pay the man for doing nothing and it's so bad for working people to be idle. Perhaps we could keep bees' – glancing at the honeycomb – 'and he could look after them. Don't you find honey expensive when they eat it at such a rate? Syrup or black treacle would be more economical.'

Mother flushed. 'Actually it was a gift, er, the honey, er, we found a whole basket filled with it, so kind.'

'I must say you are fortunate in your friends!' Our aunt gave her felt hat a spiteful tug. 'By the way, I hear you took the entire family to luncheon at that brass-founder's – the man who ran over Frances.' We gave a chorus of denials. 'Oh, I must have been mistaken. But the man drives so fast, tearing round the roads at a disgraceful speed. Anyway, I should not see too much of him, dear – a widow can't be too careful. You do cultivate the most extraordinary people – this man from Birmingham, Mrs Alexander and that Vanda woman.'

Mother was almost in tears. 'I never even met Vanda, I wouldn't know her if I saw her in the street. I admit it was careless of me to let Frances go there so much, but the child was fond of the baby. She brought it here once, but its scalp was dirty. Poor little creature, have you heard how she is getting on?'

'Can't say I have since she was removed from the Cottage Hospital and sent to Birmingham of all places. Still in plaster, I suppose. I very much doubt if she will ever be normal. You know the mother has left the district owing money. I cannot think why people are such fools as to allow credit to a woman like that.'

'Oh, Mother, it wasn't so very much: one pound seventeen at the little shop on the Walham Road and seven and nine-pence at the Red Lion for a bottle of sherry and soda-water,' Ruby said knowledgeably as she wriggled in her chair and nervously put her hand to her mouth in case she had said the wrong thing. I noticed that she was looking a little better than usual, her face softer and her little eyes brighter. Mother said afterwards that she was wearing face-powder. 'I'm sure your aunt would stop her if she knew, so I said nothing about it. She can be very unkind. Mr Blackwell has been such a good friend to us and I have so few now. Widows never seem to get asked anywhere.' Mother's face suddenly lit up. 'She doesn't know about the piano, though. She still believes it has gone away to be repaired. I said it was filled with moths.'

Fourteen

MRS HAND was in the wood-shed breaking sticks over her fat knees. She was wearing her bloodhound's face because her father had recently died. She said the old man's death was her fault because she had taken daisies into the house in winter. Other people said it was a cow's microbe that had got into a scratch in his arm and killed him, but she knew it was the daisies. We were trying to manage by burning wood on the range, because the coalman would deliver no more coal until his bill had been paid. Mother had talked to him about winding up the estate, but it had not worked this time. 'We would never have been put to this inconvenience if we lived in a better house,' Mother complained as she shivered in the drawing-room. 'If one lives in a mean house, one must expect to be treated accordingly. I shall advertise my fur coat in the *Lady*. I can manage without it quite well and the skunk collar always did smell strong, but of course I shan't mention that. Still, I'm glad I was able to wear it for John's half-term, because it was the first time I have been to Malvern since your father died, and I wouldn't have liked to let the boy down by wearing my old blue cloth coat.'

Mother sat down at the sofa table she used to write on

and started composing advertisements with the aid of a dictionary. 'I shall start with: "What offers, magnificent musquash coat?" ' she said between thoughtful bites at her pen. 'Pity I can't say "property of a titled woman", but I could put "owing to death". Better not say "sacrifice", it sounds rather Jewish.' I left Mother writing contentedly and went off to Miss Scrimpture's little house for my art lesson.

I kicked up the leaves at the side of the road as I walked slowly towards the town. Although Miss Scrimpture had taught me that twigs often have a blue light on them, my drawing and painting were not improving very rapidly, and the lessons were dull and a waste of time. I passed Louie Langston, the lanky mad boy, followed by his dog Prince. People said he did not know any better, but I felt he was sad, lolloping along with his mouth open and his knees all bent. I was trying to imagine how it felt to be him when I saw a large, old-fashioned car jerking and lurching towards me. It came to a sudden stop, then leapt forward with a roar, followed by a grating sound. As it shot past me – I could have sworn the wheels were off the ground – I saw Ruby's desperate face bent over the wheel, a mauve veil tied over her Australian hat. The new chauffeur was sitting beside her, his handsome, square face looking stark white above his dark green livery. I turned round after they had passed and noticed smoke of the darkest kind pouring from the back of the car. I imagined that a devil was sitting in the back seat – there was something nightmarish about the set faces and the car's erratic progress.

When I reached a sheltered bank, where in summer yellow and white bed-straw grew in a tangled mass, I sat down to ponder on our poorness. I felt afraid that, if it went on much longer and Mother had to keep selling things, there would eventually be nothing left to sell. How awful it would be if she wore clothes like Mrs Hand, perhaps even a man's cloth cap worn the wrong way round, firmly fixed on her head with fierce black pins. I thought about sheep's heads, pigs' trotters and cows' heels (or were they cows' wheels?), then decided that it was too late to go to Miss Scrimpture's and make Easter baskets, far better dig for celandine tubers that I could plant in a corner of the garden to surprise Mother in the spring. When I had been grubbing about the bank for some time, I saw Esmé and Clare returning from school, Esmé swinging her hat by its elastic and striding along and Clare hopping and jumping by her side. When Esmé saw me she said: 'That's good, you can take Clare home and I'll go on to the Bowmans.' I said I would, but added: 'Mother is advertising her fur coat in the *Lady*. She was writing the advertisement when I left the house, something about "What offers?"' Esmé stopped swinging her hat and put it on her head with the elastic underneath so that it stuck up like a billycock. 'I knew something would have to go,' she said thoughtfully. 'Oh well.' She shrugged her shoulders and turned back towards the town, not striding any more but walking with her head down and her hands in her pockets. I felt sorry I had mentioned Mother's coat.

When we reached The Hollies, we saw Mr Blackwell's car outside. We hurried into the house and found him in the kitchen cooking maize in a shovel to make popcorn for Toby. One moment it was a golden grain of corn and the next a puffy white flake, four times the size. We gathered round the stove, still wearing our overcoats, and ate the corn as if we were famished hens, while Mr Blackwell told us how he used to make popcorn in his mother's kitchen when he was a boy and about the tiger-nuts and liquorice boot-laces he used to buy from a little shop on the corner of the poor street where he lived. 'Toby, I must start you on liquorice boot-laces, I must have eaten miles of them,' he said cheerfully as he tipped the last shovel full of popcorn on to a kitchen plate. 'I'm afraid I've let the fire get a bit low, but I'll make it up if you show me where the coal-bucket is; I can only see wood here. I'm an expert furnace-man.' And he raked the fire, the red glowing on his narrow face. I was wondering what to say when Clare piped out: 'There isn't any coal because the coalman's so beastly, Mother's furious with him.' I hurriedly picked up the larger pieces of wood and flung them on to the stove. Mr Black-well absent-mindedly hooked the rings into place as he said quietly: 'I know all about beastly coalmen and beastly grocers,' and, after leaving his kind regards to Mother, he left the house. I was furious with Clare and snapped at her: 'You made everyone miserable, just when we were all so happy. Don't you know being poor is a very private thing?' I crossly dragged off her overcoat and hung it in the hall, but then I noticed her poor little jersey sleeve with no hand coming from it and gave her a friendly push, telling her to eat the popcorn while it was still hot. Toby sat on the kitchen mat pulling his shoe-laces and saying to himself: 'I don't think sweet laces will be strong enough for me.'

Mother returned from the village, where she had been posting her letter to the *Lady*. She was wearing her fur coat and I guessed she was planning to wear it as much as possible while she still owned it. She appeared quite light-hearted until she took off her beehive hat. Then I could see that her eyes were inflamed, but she assured us that it was the wind. She asked if Mr Blackwell had been, because she had seen a giant marrow and some pomegranates in the hall.

We were not long without coal. The coalman relented. At least, he arrived with a whole ton of coal, enough to last the entire winter, and said we were not to dream of paying for it, it was a present. Unlike Mr Blackwell, he enjoyed our gratitude and sat in the kitchen lapping it up with his tea. In spite of him letting us have coal for nothing, I still felt he was beastly, but Mother said he must have been suffering from his liver: 'I remember at the time I thought him a bad colour in spite of the coal-dust on his face, and his eyeballs looked quite yellow. Poor man, I expect he was too ill to recognize me and it has been worrying him ever since.'

It was more than fortunate that the coal crisis was over, because there was only one offer of five pounds for Mother's coat. She decided not to sell it and to forget that the skunk collar smelt. We had another pleasant surprise in December when the lawyers sent our monthly cheque. It appeared that our mattress shares were paying a higher dividend than usual and the lawyers had let the money mount up to £25 so that we could have a windfall for Christmas. Mother kept saying how honest they were, because she wouldn't have known anything about it if they hadn't sent the cheque. Then she turned to Esmé and asked nervously: 'Do you think it would matter if we didn't mention this bonus to Polly? I'd like her to think I'd been managing well while she has been away. Although it isn't really true, I'd rather she didn't know. I suppose I shall have to admit about selling the piano, though.' Polly was due home from Switzerland for a month's holiday at Christmas, the first holiday since she had left home.

In a morning session with the Lawrences it was decided that Polly at seventeen was old enough to travel across London by herself. In any case, it was unlikely that other girls would not be making the same journey. If Mother had had to escort her home, it would have meant her spending a night in London and leaving us alone in the house. 'But, suppose she does not catch the right train, she may end up at Penzance,' Mother said fearfully, although she was relieved that it was considered unnecessary for her to stay in London alone. Aunt Lawrence reassured her firmly: 'If the girl can't manage a simple journey of that sort after living abroad for nearly a year, she must be a fool and we have wasted our money. Talking of fools, what do you think of Ruby taking up driving a motor-car? Too nervous to ride but wants to do a damn dangerous thing like driving. Jackson, the new chauffeur, you know, says she'll learn in time, but he does not consider the Napier suitable for her – too heavy and old-fashioned, he says. Well, we certainly can't afford two cars and the Napier suits us well enough.' To our astonishment, Ruby broke her mother's monologue with: 'Oh, Mother, it would be cheaper to have a new car. That old thing eats up petrol and oil.'

The driving lessons had quite changed Ruby. Even if she did look so distraught at the wheel, they seemed to have given her a new assurance. She would chatter away about changing gears and double-declutching: 'Jackson says I'll be quite good when I get over my nervousness, it's just that I lack confidence. And, after all, the car is too heavy for me – I can't even turn the starting-handle. I understand about the gears perfectly, although I can't go into reverse yet (that's driving backwards, you know: very difficult). But Jackson says it's stopping and starting on hills that is the very devil.' She laughed, then glanced slyly at her mother, who fortunately was not listening, but telling Mother how to make cheap mincemeat for pies with carrots instead of sultanas, while Mother was politely looking into space and thinking of something else.

Grace, with the gold band that imprisoned her teeth gleaming in the morning light, pranced into the room, wearing a new riding habit of dark grey cloth. 'Mummy, look,' she cried as she posed in front of the window, 'see how well it fits. That old idiot in the market-place knows how to cut. It's nice, isn't it? And the jacket looks marvellous from the back.' She turned her slim back to be admired and her mother went to her to tweak and pull and pat. Grace was her favourite child.

I followed Grace to her bedroom to help get her feet out of her riding-boots. I tugged and she laughed and I eventually fell over backwards, clutching a shining black boot. She said she had asked me to her bedroom because she wanted to tell me something very funny. She sat on her bed, admiring her legs as she put them into fawn lisle stockings. 'It's about Ruby,' she said as she adjusted her suspenders. 'Do you know why she is crazy about driving?' I shook my head and she smiled mysteriously. 'I thought you wouldn't. Well, the truth is she's all spoony about Jackson. She hangs about the garage all day, even helps him clean the car, and it's Jackson this and Jackson that every time she opens her mouth. Mummy hasn't noticed and I'm not saying a word. I just want to see what happens. I'm sure those driving lessons absolutely terrify poor Jackson. He's had to grab the steering-wheel from her several times or they would have been killed, or at least had an accident, so old Pat tells me. I wouldn't want that to happen, of course, but I'm hoping Daddy will catch them kissing in the car, or something like that.' She rolled about the bed, waving her legs in the air as she laughed. 'Oh dear, poor old Ruby. She really is a scream, and she's plastering her face with powder. Have you noticed?' I said that Mother had, but she thought it an improvement. Grace left the bed and wandered to the mirror and looked intently at her pretty face. 'I'm sure your mother would; after all, she uses rather a lot of face-powder herself. Someone was saying only the other day that she rouges. It isn't true, is it?' She gathered her gold-brown hair into a rough bun and admired the effect as I cried indignantly: 'Of course it isn't true. Mother has the most beautiful natural complexion, far better than yours will ever be.' I stumped from the room and slammed the door after me, but I stood still when I reached the head of the stairs and wished I had not lost my temper. Esmé would have snubbed her, perhaps even suggesting that

Aunt Lawrence rouged. I couldn't help smiling at the thought.

Except for John, who was still at school, we all assembled on the station an hour before Polly's train was due. We hung about watching other trains coming and going and people meeting and parting. Every time a train passed Mother held Toby's coat-tails in case he was sucked underneath. I saw a bent old woman being helped along the platform by her two daughters. So slow she was and bent forward so that her chin almost touched her stomach, and as she tottered past people looked at her with different expressions on their faces. The older ones had a look of horrified pity, but the younger ones appeared disgusted and amused. She could not control the spit that was dribbling from her mouth, and every now and again one of the daughters would wipe her lips with a man's handkerchief, staring ahead with the self-conscious, pained faces like the parents of idiot children wear. As I watched the old woman, I realized for the first time that one day I would turn into an old woman and crumble away like a dead leaf. I'd vaguely thought that grown-up people always stayed more or less the same age. I knew that Mother had once been a child, because I had seen photographs of her and she often mentioned her childhood, but I didn't really connect that child with Mother. It seemed impossible that Aunt Lawrence's hair had not always been grey and that Shakespeare's dome-like head had once been covered with bright hair. I tried to imagine Mr Blackwell as a small child minus his moustache, but it was impossible. I was so engrossed in my thoughts that I did not see the others rush forward as the London train steamed in, and was startled to hear the sudden commotion all around me. A man almost knocked me over as he hurried past with a basket-work case, and a woman with her hat on the back of her head ran after him shouting: 'Bert, Bert, you've dropped yer ticket.' Then I saw a radiant Polly being kissed by Mother and I slowly went towards them, feeling strangely shy, because Polly had turned into a woman. The brim of her hat was as large as Mother's and I could hardly see her legs because her green velour coat was so long. It wasn't only Polly who had changed; apparently we had too. She was exclaiming over how Toby had grown, then it was Clare dressed like a schoolgirl that caught her attention, then Esmé. 'Esmé, I'd forgotten your enormous brown eyes. And Frances! Heavens, how tall and thin you have grown.'

We crowded into a station cab with Polly's trunks piled on the roof and all stared at her. Mother said: 'I do hope you don't find the house too poky after being away so long. It's a shock to me even if I'm away only a few hours.'

Polly peeled off her kid gloves and examined her smooth hands. 'Oh no, Mother, you can't think how I'm longing to be home and sit before a real fire instead of those ghastly stoves. I'm afraid these gloves are a little small, but I do like them to be well fitting.' Esmé and I glanced down at our woollen gloves – mine had a thumb missing. Clare said: 'Do you know, the girls at school are awfully nice about my hand. I thought they would say things about it, but only a few did, and I told them I lost it in an aeroplane accident when I was flying with my friend, Mr Blackwell. Have you met Mr Blackwell, Polly? He's our great friend.' Esmé smiled. 'I wondered how that story about the aeroplane got round. You are a fantastic little liar, Clare.' 'I'm not a liar,' Clare said indignantly. 'It isn't a lie, because it could so easily be true. Mr Blackwell has promised to take me in an aeroplane one day, and I expect there will be an accident when he does.'

Mother said: 'Stop talking so much, child. I want to hear about Polly's journey. Did you have a rough crossing?' Polly's description of her journey lasted until we reached

173

The Hollies. As we entered the house, Mother said in a low voice to Esmé: 'Isn't it fortunate about the coal? Suppose the poor girl had returned to her home longing for a coal fire and the grates had been empty. Hum, I wonder what Aunt Lawrence will think of her. She's bound to be round this evening.'

Fifteen

AUNT LAWRENCE did not come round that evening or the next day. We did not miss her, because the new Polly that had returned took all our thoughts and attention. She astonished us the first morning by asking if she could have breakfast in bed. It would be such heaven to lie in bed and and not hear a single school bell, she said. I took up her breakfast neatly arranged, with a napkin covering the old stained tray. We were eating the best pink bacon now and never ordered the striped that Polly used to make us buy, but she didn't notice. There was a small pile of books by her bed, two in French and one in German. But her nightgown! It was lovely, all embroidered round the neck and sleeves. When she noticed me admiring it, she said she had made it herself and she would make me one if there was time before she returned. We could walk into the town and buy some fine lawn this morning. No thought about the money to buy it with. I remembered the time she had made us wear night-gowns made from worn-out sheets without even any lace to decorate them – we used to call them 'our shrouds'.

We walked into the town together, Esmé slipping off on the way to do the shopping. We thought it would be better if we kept the fact that we now dealt with different shops from Polly. When we came to Grey & Friend, the big drapers, I stopped to gaze at the three wax women wearing satin gowns in the centre of the window. There was a hand-painted card decorated with bells, saying: 'For the Festive Season' placed beside them and the rest of the window was crammed with shining blouses. Some were 'Chic' and others 'Good Value'. I was extremely fond of the three wax women, whose clothes were changed at least once a month. Once, when they had been dressed in maids' uniforms, their faces had worn an air of hurt embarrassment and it was a relief when they were put into winter coats, 'Warm but Smart'. Polly gave the window one glance and said: 'Oh dear!' and sailed into the shop, where money raced round the ceilings in small containers. I could have watched it all day, but Polly said it was an old-fashioned system. She had been to a shop in London called Harrods, where they had lifts.

On our way home Mr Blackwell passed us, driving to-wards the town. He was driving as he often did, lolling over one door, and he gave a friendly wave. Polly frowned: 'I seem to remember that man. Isn't he the one we used to call "that brass-founder"? I told her about him and how he had become our friend, but she couldn't understand how this had come about. She asked what the Lawrences thought about the friendship and I said I didn't know. I preferred not to repeat the remark that 'widows can't be too careful'. To change the subject, I told her about Ruby's driving lessons, which she thought even more extraordinary.

When two days had passed and there had been no Lawrences to welcome Polly home, Mother became worried and hurt. Every time our gate banged she looked up hope-fully, but it was always one of us coming or going, or the milkman. Mr Blackwell did not call either, most likely be-cause he was shy of meeting Polly, but we missed him. Then, when we were laying the table for tea, one of the Tower Hill

176

maids came to the door with a note for Mother, asking her to come to the house immediately, alone. No mention of Polly, the note definitely said 'alone'. The maid waited and escorted our bewildered mother to Tower Hill. They sloshed away in the rainy darkness while we sat in the warm dining-room eating plum cake made from the left-overs of the Christmas cake. Polly had lost her interest in household management and economy and failed to notice that our food had become much more luxurious and that our porridge was now made with milk, not water. It was our clothes that she worried about now and, when she wasn't stitching away at my night-gown, she was turning hems up and down, removing grease spots, pressing pleats and supervising our mending.

Esmé and I were bent over our boring mending when Mother returned an hour or so later. Still wearing her overcoat, she burst into the dining-room with a stricken expression on her face. She stood there and said: 'Children,' then in muffled jerks she spoke of Ruby: 'I know you all think of her as a ridiculous, plain girl, it's true she is, but I remember her as a baby and she was the dearest little thing, the first baby I'd ever known well. Aunt Lawrence was so proud of her then, but after Charles came something seemed to go wrong and that enchanting baby has turned into the Ruby we now know. That poor girl, she's had no love.' The thought of Ruby's lack of love brought on such a violent fit of sobbing that we were convinced she was dead.

Polly went to Mother and peeled her from her coat, saying gently: 'Poor Mother, are you trying to tell us that Ruby has had a terrible accident in that car? Is that what you are so upset about?'

'No, it's much worse than that,' Mother cried wildly. 'I hardly like to tell you children, but Ruby's run away, completely disappeared. You see, it's really very shocking, but they fear she's with Jackson, the young chauffeur. He has been dismissed with a month's pay. It seems your uncle saw him behaving in a most familiar way with Ruby and dismissed him on the spot. Very sensible of him, of course. But to think of poor Ruby running after him like that, a girl with her background, only twenty and so young for her age in many ways!' We waited breathlessly while Mother fumbled for her handkerchief and blew her nose. 'They have no idea where she is, although she left a note saying she had gone to join him. Such a bald and shameless note, they said, but I didn't read it. She left it in her father's slipper-box, of all places – it might not have been found for days if his corn had not been troubling him. The family are quite broken, not broken-hearted, but broken.' Mother paused in her torrent of words and said thoughtfully: 'Perhaps that's the saddest part; it's the disgrace they care about, not the loss of their daughter. Of course they are trying to keep it quiet, but Uncle had to make inquiries at the railway station to ask if she had been seen buying a ticket. The stationmaster remembered seeing her on the platform and thought she had taken the Birmingham train, but was not sure. She could have only had a few pounds on her, but she remembered to take her jewellery – not that it's worth much, just a few girlish trinkets. If she had waited another year, she would have had a pearl necklace on her twenty-first birthday. Poor, silly girl! They say they will never take her back because of Grace – they can't have her contaminated. Ruby has made her bed and must sleep in it. I said it would be better if she didn't, but they wouldn't listen to anything I said.' Mother's wailing voice suddenly ceased and she sank exhaustedly into a chair. The stricken look left her face and she smiled at us quite calmly. 'I'm so glad, darlings, that we can't afford a chauffeur and that you girls are safe.'

John came home the following day, but that didn't prevent Aunt Lawrence coming and shutting herself up with Mother in the drawing-room for nearly two hours. Except for Uncle Lawrence and Old Nanny, she had no one except Mother to discuss Ruby's disappearance with. Ruby had sent a postcard from Coventry saying: 'I'm very happy here. Please don't try to find me,' so of course Uncle Lawrence was motoring to Coventry the next day. Aunt Lawrence said: 'The girl must be mad, telling us where she is and then asking not to be followed. I think she's hoping that one of us will take her home. If you ask me, she's homesick and crying her eyes out.' They had changed their minds about Ruby sleeping in the bed she had made and had decided to put her in a cottage miles from anywhere in Nanny's charge.

As Aunt Lawrence was leaving, Mr Blackwell arrived, carrying a huge black turkey in one hand and a great basket of fruit in the other. Mother introduced them in the hall and Mr Blackwell said nervously: 'I'm afraid I can't shake hands, I'm rather loaded up,' and we heard our aunt reply in an icy voice: 'So I see.' Then the front door slammed.

John rushed into the hall to welcome him. Mr Blackwell said: 'I say, old boy, do you know where I can hang this bird?' and, as they went into the larder, Mother called after them: 'I know you hate to be thanked, Mr Blackwell, but you can't bring a great bird like that into the house and escape.' She added to us in a low voice: 'Aunt was so cold to him. You should have seen the expression on her face when she saw what he was carrying. I'm afraid she thought it wrong of me to take presents from a man. I really don't know how it started. Oh yes, when Frances was ill, he brought her little gifts, and now they have grown larger and larger.' Polly said quietly: 'I must say I was rather surprised when I heard that Mr Blackwell had become a family friend, but I didn't know he was bringing things to the house.' She looked slightly pained as she bent over her sewing and there was a strained silence.

When John and Mr Blackwell entered the room Polly was introduced to him. They shook hands in a formal way. Polly turned down the corners of her mouth when he said: 'Pleased to meet you,' and I could see she was missing the kindly and amusing man who lived behind his big moustache. He appeared even more enormous than usual in our small, square rooms and, as if conscious of this, curled himself up when he was sitting, wrapping his legs round the chair legs. Mother thanked him for the turkey and asked if he would like to share it with us on Christmas Day: 'It will be a simple meal, with the girls helping to serve, but we would love to have you.' She smiled very charmingly and after a few shy protests the invitation was accepted, and we could tell he was touched and pleased at being asked. He left soon after that, and as we heard him drive away, we asked Polly what she thought of him. She said she didn't quite know, she would tell us when she knew him better. 'You see, it's a bit of a shock suddenly finding a man like that, and such a large one, coming to our house in such an intimate way, almost like a relation. I think I like him, though.' She added thoughtfully: 'I wonder if he will carve the turkey.'

Charles drove his father to Coventry on Christmas Eve, but they didn't succeed in finding Ruby. Most reluctantly they made inquiries at the police station. It must have been an agony to Uncle Lawrence to admit that he didn't know what name his daughter was using, and that she was probably living with a dismissed servant. Aunt Lawrence said he had aged twenty years.

She arrived on Christmas morning, when the house was smelling deliciously of roasting turkey, stood sniffing like a dog in the hall and said: 'I thought we gave you a brace of pheasants.' Mother turned away and took off her large white apron and called to Polly to take over in the kitchen. 'Yes, Aunt, and we are very glad to have them. They are hanging in the larder because we like them high – er – just right for Sunday, I thought. But Mr Blackwell gave us a turkey, you know. You must have noticed he was carrying one when I introduced you.'

When they had disappeared into the drawing-room, where Ruby's – and perhaps Mother's – behaviour was discussed in private, we all gathered in the kitchen to help cook. Even Toby grated breadcrumbs until he grated his own skin, and Clare played to us on the pretty Swiss musical box that Polly had brought back for her.

Aunt Lawrence had gone by the time Mr Blackwell arrived, much to Mother's relief. After suitable Christmas greetings had been exchanged, he asked John to come out to the car with him, because there were a few little things that he needed to bring in. The few little things turned out to be a case of wine, all sorts of delicious things for dessert, a tiny green bicycle for Toby and a gramophone with an assortment of records. 'I asked the girl for a mixed bag of classical and cheerful records and left it to her.' We were all extraordinarily happy – and it wasn't only due to the presents: there seemed to be a sort of glow in the air and, as we breathed it, we glowed ourselves. Even when the dinner was over and cracker papers were piled on the plates, we still felt it as we washed up in the kitchen.

When we returned to the drawing-room, there were Mother and Mr Blackwell sitting either side of the fire like married people, but their conversation was formal enough. They were discussing Burne-Jones's paintings and drawings in the Birmingham Art Gallery. Mother admired them immensely, Mr Blackwell was not so enthusiastic. 'I expect the paintings are very fine,' he said as he gazed into the fire with a far-away expression on his face, 'but what I really like are the birds in those glass cases with their great white wings; they appeal to me enormously.' He left at about six, taking John with him to eat another Christmas dinner. His staff would be disappointed if he didn't eat one at home: 'They expect me to sit at that long, empty table, pulling crackers by myself. I shall be extremely glad of your company, John.' As they drove away Polly remarked to herself: 'So he did carve! I thought he would.'

Uncle Lawrence and Charles found Ruby on Boxing Day. Charles told me how it happened. She was staying in a little terraced house with an outside lavatory. The lavatory seemed to be the last straw for the Lawrences, who referred to it repeatedly. When they arrived at the address the police had given them, they peered through the lace-curtained window and saw Ruby sitting in state on a shiny sofa before a flaming fire, drinking something from a steaming teacup and reading *Home Chat*. She didn't look at all as if she wanted to be rescued. A plump, middle-aged woman answered the door, guessed who they were immediately and said in a shaking voice: 'Oh dear, we thought you might come. My son's not at home at the moment, just gone round to his aunty's to see to her gas stove, which is behaving in ever such a queer way. Miss Ruby's here, although I don't know what she'll say about me letting you in.'

Uncle Lawrence didn't wait to be let in, he marched straight into the parlour while Charles was still listening to Jackson's mother on the doorstep. Charles heard Ruby cry sharply: 'You needn't think you're going to take me home. I won't go with you. You can't order me about any more, because I'm married.' Uncle Lawrence turned to the mother standing in the door and asked: 'Is this true?' and she agreed that it was. Miss Ruby and her Jim had been married by special licence on Christmas Eve. 'In ever such a hurry they were. I suppose the neighbours will talk, but it can't be helped. I'm sure they'll be ever so happy together, although Miss Ruby isn't the girl we expected our son to marry; but I'm sure she'll

182

make him a good wife. She's affectionate, you see. Not much of a looker, but ever so loving.'

Uncle Lawrence had to be shown the certificate before he would believe the marriage had taken place. Then he swore he would have it annulled because Ruby's age was incorrectly given as twenty-one. Jackson returned while he was storming round the hot little room and Ruby rushed to him and, clutching his arm, begged him not to let them take her away. Charles said he felt awfully sorry for her and wished they hadn't interfered.

After storming, Uncle Lawrence pleaded, then suddenly went grey in the face and had to be escorted to the outside lavatory. He stayed away some time and in his absence Charles was able to talk to Ruby and Jackson in a more friendly way. Jackson told him that he had a temporary job in a bicycle factory and he felt it was better at the moment to continue living with his mother. 'You see, Miss Ruby – I mean Ruby – doesn't know about housekeeping yet and Mother can teach her. You're happy here, aren't you, Ruby?' he asked. She assured him that she was and Charles told me she really did look happy. He asked her if there was anything she needed and she said rather shyly: 'Yes, a trousseau, underclothes and things. The girls here have such pretty ones, quite different to the kind Mother always chose for me. And one or two dresses, pink ones. Jim likes me in pink, but I've only one pink blouse and I can't wear it all the time.' Jackson said: 'Yes, she looks nice in pink, it gives her a bit of colour. Mother's giving her Iron Jelloids, thinks she's a bit anaemic.'

Charles said he would see what could be done about the trousseau. He might be able to give her one as a wedding present and he'd get Old Nanny to send on all her clothes. 'But not the flannel night-gowns,' Ruby insisted, 'or the bloomers.'

Uncle Lawrence returned in a deflated condition and ordered Charles to drive him home immediately, as he was feeling far from well. He took up his brown bowler and tottered from the house without another word to Ruby, but Charles kissed his sister and shook hands with her husband before he left.

He told me all this as we sat on a gate together on New Year's Day, his gun propped up against a post while the rooks he had intended to shoot flew slowly overhead, cawing with their rusty voices in the still, damp air. Charles appeared to be quite obsessed with Ruby; he was glad to talk about her because he was forbidden to mention her at home. 'It was extraordinary seeing her in that poor little house, sitting behind lace curtains, living on lacy dreams and Iron Jelloids. I'm sure the mother waits on her hand and foot and Jackson's fond of her. I suppose he married her for what he can get out of it; all the same, I think he's kind and will look after her. I hope Father will eventually do something for them, he'll have to. She'll have a few hundreds when she's twenty-one, money her godmother left her, not much, but I suppose they could start something with it, a shop or garage, perhaps.' He batted his eyes thoughtfully and added: 'I know no one will agree with me, but I'm glad she's gone off with Jackson. She led such a wretched life at home. She looks different now, softer and not so jerky. Even if Jackson lets her down eventually, she will have had some sort of happiness, poor girl.' As he talked, he absent-mindedly cracked hazel-nuts between the palms of his hands and handed them to me, occasionally eating one himself. The gate was beginning to cut into my behind, but I was proud to be sitting there in the dusk with Charles.

Sixteen

MOTHER behaved in a strange way for days before she told us she was going to marry Mr Blackwell. She broke it to us when the hall was full of trunks, the day before Polly and John returned to their schools. She just remarked that trunks reminded her of changes and there was going to be a great change for the better in our lives. 'I shall be marrying Mr Blackwell – Edward – in a few weeks and we will all be living at Springfield with him. Don't look at me like that, Polly. I don't care what you say, I intend to marry him for all your sakes, as much as for mine.' Then she rushed upstairs with her skirts flying out behind and slammed her bedroom door. Polly sank on to the hall bench. 'I wasn't looking at her like anything. Why pick on me? Anyway, I knew Mr Blackwell intended to marry Mother when he carved the turkey, and she's been so queer ever since – as if she was floating about on the moon.' She ran her fingers through her curly fringe until it looked like the bobbles on old people's mantelshelves and wandered off to the kitchen, where she relieved her feelings by rattling the fire-irons and needlessly raking the range. She had been upset for the last two days, since she had heard that Grace was to accompany her to Montreux and that Aunt Lawrence was travelling as far as Victoria

Station with them. The rest of us humped ourselves on the trunks, thinking our own thoughts, too appalled to talk. It was not the thought of Mr Blackwell that shocked us, but of living in his house with all those servants and carpets and nothing of ours there. Clare broke the silence by saying: 'There will be huge eiderdowns on our beds and we'll see Mr Blackwell walking about the landings in his dressing-gown.' Toby said: 'Yes, and we'll never know our ways there, we'll all be lost.' That was just how we felt, that we'd all be lost. After a time John said it was the shock that was making us depressed and it was only a matter of getting used to the idea of living at Springfield. 'It's really an awfully good thing for us, particularly for Mother. She's always hated living here, and Mr Blackwell is the kindest man, we couldn't have a better step-father.' He smiled at that. 'Lord, I hadn't thought, we'll have to call him "Father"!'

We none of us mentioned Mother's intended marriage when she crept into the dining-room to share our cold supper, but she brought up the subject herself when we were clearing away. She was ineffectually dabbing at the tablecloth with a small brush meant for sweeping away crumbs when she said: 'You won't mention it to the Lawrences, will you? I'll tell them myself in a few days.' We assured her that we wouldn't mention it to anyone. Then John told her how pleased he was, she couldn't have chosen a better husband. Esmé and I awkwardly kissed her and said we felt the same, but Polly left the room with her back bent over a heavily-loaded tray.

When Esmé and I were in bed, we felt disturbed and home-sick. 'I'll miss those marks on the ceiling,' Esmé said, gazing up at them fondly before she blew the candle out. I said: 'It'll be electricity there and a maid will call us in the morning with those big brass cans filled with hot water.' 'Yes,' Esmé agreed, 'with a little towel folded on top. And she'll draw the curtains and be respectful.' I suddenly started to cry and gasped out: 'Oh, Esmé, have you realized? Those awful skin chairs will be ours, we'll have to live with them.' Esmé said impatiently: 'Do shut up and go to sleep. If you feel so badly about the chairs, you had better give them a Christian burial.'

We seemed to spend most of the following day on the station, first seeing Polly, Aunt Lawrence and Grace on to a train, then John. Just before her train left, Polly jumped out of the carriage, rushed to Mother and flung her arms round her, whispering: 'Send me a photograph of Springfield, I'd like the other girls to see it. Sorry I was beastly about it.'

Aunt Lawrence hustled her back into the carriage, where she stood by the window looking strangely childish, waving as the train steamed out.

A few days later, when Mother was standing on a stool in front of the china cupboard sorting out the china and muttering: 'Not worth keeping, only rubbish, badly cracked. Hum, your father's moustache-cup may come in useful,' I thought I heard the front gate slam and went to see if anyone was about. There was Aunt Lawrence, poking about in the holly hedge with her walking-stick because she thought she had seen a sleeping hedgehog, which turned out to be a ball of dry, dead grass. 'Dirty little creatures, covered in fleas. Can't have them near the house. Well, dear, is your mother in?'

I led her to the kitchen, where Mother was still perched on her stool. 'Hard at it, I see,' Aunt Lawrence remarked complacently as she seated herself in the wicker chair, crossing her slim legs to display the knitted diamond pattern on her stockings. Mother climbed down and gave the pink cheek a pecking kiss and asked how she had got on in London. 'Oh, quite well, quite well. I saw the girls off safely. I must say that Madame Helga seems a very good sort of woman and the parents I saw looked decent enough. One woman was wearing a beautiful sable coat. Oh yes, I must tell you a funny thing. This will interest you, Frances,' and she fixed me with her pussy-blue eyes. 'That Vanda woman was on the station and she came up and spoke to me in the most friendly way. I should have thought she'd have been embarrassed. I must say she was looking very well turned out, I wouldn't have recognized her. Anyway, she congratulated me on Ruby's marriage. We had to announce it in *The Times* to stop gossip. "Married quietly", you know. I invented the parents' Christian names because there was no way of finding out their real ones. Desmond and Olivia I called them, although Fred and Gladys is far more likely.'

I waited patiently to hear what she had to say about Vanda. I never liked to inquire about Jane, because I was afraid of what I might hear, afraid even to think of her, remembering how she had looked with the blood on her mouth on that terrible last afternoon. Aunt Lawrence returned to the subject after rambling on about Ruby for a bit. 'Yes, there was Vanda all dressed in black – a beautifully cut coat and skirt, but black. Of course, when I saw her dressed like that, I asked how the baby was, expecting to hear it was dead. But she assured me that the little thing is out of its plaster cast and, although she will have to have treatment, will completely recover. The child has been living with one of the doctors for some time. It seems that he and his wife have taken a great fancy to her and want to adopt her. The woman talked a lot of nonsense about not wanting to be parted from her baby, but, as she intends to travel to India in a few weeks, she thinks she may consent. A wonderful thing for the child, but I'm sure her mother's up to no good. She hadn't a penny to bless herself with when she was here.'

Now I'd heard the good news about Jane, I thought I might as well leave the kitchen to give Mother a chance to tell Aunt

Lawrence her news, but when I reached the door I heard my aunt make an appalling suggestion. She had got the idea into her head that I should stay at Tower Hill. 'She settled down very well when she stayed before and I must admit I find the house lonely without the girls. She could come right away. Do you remember how you used to enjoy cleaning out the birds, Frances?' I answered bleakly as I swung on the doorhandle: 'Yes, Aunt Lawrence,' giving Mother an anguished glance, which she didn't see – her heavy lids were drooping more than usual.

Aunt Lawrence uncrossed her diamond-decorated legs and got up briskly. 'That's settled then. I'll send the dog-cart round tomorrow morning.' Mother opened her eyes wide and said in a far-away voice: 'Oh no, Aunt, it's out of the question. I can't have the children more separated than they are already. When there is going to be such a change in their lives, it's far better for them to be together as much as possible. Partings are so unsettling, don't you agree?'

'I have no idea what you are talking about,' Aunt Lawrence said irritably, as she pushed her capable hands into grey leather gloves. 'I hope you haven't taken up some silly notion about leaving this house.'

Mother said in a rush: 'Yes, that's exactly what's happening. You see, we don't need it any more, because we are all going to Springfield. I'm sure you won't be surprised to hear that Mr Blackwell – Edward – and I are getting married almost immediately.'

Aunt Lawrence let out an incredulous 'No!' – it sounded like air hissing out of a bicycle tyre. Then she barked: 'Does this man know how many children you have?'

'Well, I haven't hidden any. I suppose he can count.'

'But, my dear, have you thought what you are doing? A self-made man! It will break your uncle's heart, his only brother's child considering such an unsuitable marriage. No education or background at all, I should imagine. A completely self-made man.'

Mother snapped: 'Self-made man! I always think that's such a silly expression – and rather irreligious if you come to think of it. I shall be proud to marry Edward and he'll be a wonderful father to the children. Oh, I'm sick and tired of being a widow. How would you like to live in a wretched little house and have all the worry and responsibilities I've had? And the children: think of the difference my marriage will make to them. Ponies and horses, good schools, aeroplanes.' Mother's voice rose. 'Yes, aeroplanes. Edward's planning to start an aerodrome or aeroplane factory, something like that, and John will go in with him when he leaves school.'

'I should keep him off aeroplanes unless you want to be a widow again. Very well, dear, there is no need to get so excited. I can see you've made up your mind to take this step. After all, you haven't any social position to lose.' As I saw my aunt's vigorous back disappearing down the path, I thought: 'When you're plodding through the fields on your horses, Mother will be sailing through the clouds in her own aeroplane,' and I had a vivid picture of her wearing a flowing evening dress, driving her own silver aeroplane, coloured chiffon scarves trailing behind.

When I returned to the kitchen, Mother sank into the creaking wicker chair: 'Goodness, I'm glad that's over. Now Edward can see the vicar about putting up the banns. I thought it would be unkind to mention Ruby's marriage, although I almost had to bite my tongue not to. I think I will give all the china to Mrs Hand. Her husband gets drunk sometimes and breaks everything up, so it'll come in useful. I'll just keep your father's moustache-cup.'

Seventeen

I N S P I T E of Uncle Lawrence's heart being broken over his only niece contemplating marriage to a self-made brass-founder, he gave her away most cheerfully. As a matter of fact, I think he was relieved to hand the responsibility of Mother and her six children over to Mr Blackwell, and he looked very foxy and smiling as he escorted her up the aisle of the village church. I could almost see a red, bushy tail triumphantly waving from the back of his well-cut dark suit. There were just the five of us children in the front pew and Aunt Lawrence and Old Nanny in the one behind. Mrs Hand was snuffling somewhere in the background and one or two village women stood by the open door. We listened to Mother and Mr Blackwell solemnly repeating the things the clergyman told them to say, and the air was full of the smell that comes out of sideboards when you open the cupboard doors.

They stood so still, Mother and Mr Blackwell, before the flower-decorated altar, and their voices sounded strange and far away. I was glad when they disappeared through a side door and the service was over, for it was rather alarming seeing them so unlike their usual selves, Mr Blackwell's oddly small head bowed and Mother trembling-voiced and dressed in grey cloth and dark fur, clothes I'd never seen before.

191

The Lawrences followed them through the mysterious side door and we self-consciously trailed out of the church, past the village women and into the churchyard, where a wintry sun was shining.

We were all sitting on a friendly tomb playing 'I spy' when Old Nanny found us and said that we had no respect for our bottoms or the dead. She wanted us to go into the vestry and kiss the bride and groom, but we felt too shy and went and stood by the cars outside the church, hoping no one would notice us. Besides feeling embarrassed that it was our mother's wedding-day, we felt unsettled and lost, not knowing which of the two cars to sit in or whether the little reception we had heard about was to be held at the Lawrences' or Springfield, or even if we were to be included.

Then the wedding party emerged from a small arched door and, although their clothes were still different, they were their usual selves and spoke with their usual voices. John went forward and kissed Mother and shook hands with Mr Blackwell and we all followed suit in spite of the village people looking on. Charles appeared from nowhere and drove us to Tower Hill in Mr Blackwell's Hispano-Suiza, the wedding party slowly following behind in the stately old Napier.

We ate wedding cake and drank our first glasses of champagne and, just when we were beginning to think weddings were not such bad things after all, Mother and Mr Blackwell were rushing off to spend a month in Madeira, a place for wine and winter honeymoons.

Old Nanny came to look after us while Mother was away. We continued to live at The Hollies, and Mrs Hand cooked us meat in stiff salty gravy and puddings that were so heavy we could hardly lift our spoons. Nanny offered to do some of the cooking, but we couldn't bear to think of her crumbling into our food and had to pretend we liked Mrs Hand's cooking, although, besides being so unappetizing anyway, it managed to taste of the paraffin that we used in the lamps. Strange women from the building estate came and spoke to us through their false teeth, asking how we liked our new father and if we were lonely without our mother. They said it was a shame. The coalman called and told us not to forget him, because he had always treated us well, and the butcher hoped he wouldn't lose our custom when we moved to Springfield. 'I always treated your mother very fair,' he said. 'I didn't want her little family to go short.' And the grocer from his shop that smelt of cats came too, bringing peardrops of all colours, even mauve.

Sometimes Aunt Lawrence arrived with her little black dog and sat in the kitchen talking to Old Nanny about Ruby and Grace. Uncle Lawrence had bought her a new hunter, white with little grey specks – flea-bitten, I think it is called – but she still missed her girls, even Ruby, whom she used not to care for. I heard her tell Old Nanny that, if only she could get Uncle Lawrence out of the house for the day, she would ask Charles to drive her to Coventry. 'I want to see for myself how she is living. I put a little money in between her clothes when we packed her trunks; I hope she discovered it. And some of her flannel night-gowns – you remember how she feels the cold.' She would read Grace's letters out loud, while Nanny dozed by the stove, her steel knitting-needles, entwined with grey wool, lying idle in her chalky hands.

Before she left, Mother had said we could visit Springfield if we liked, but we were scared. One afternoon, when I was feeling particularly bored, I did venture there, but the maids didn't even know who I was at first. I'd wanted to explore the upstairs part of the house and choose which bedroom I would sleep in, but the parlourmaid seemed so hostile that I said that I'd only come to play in the garden. I gingerly walked up and down the velvety lawn and couldn't believe it was ours. I wandered round the lonely stableyard and heard Mr Blackwell's one horse stamping in its stall. I would have liked to have climbed up into the loft, but there was a rumble of men's voices coming from it – the gardener and the groom were playing cards up there. 'Where the 'ell did you get that queen from?' came floating down as soon as I put a foot on the stone steps. A boy in a dark-blue uniform rode a bicycle into the yard and rang the large bell outside the back door, and from the orchard I could hear someone sharpening a scythe. I thought how strange it would be getting used to different sounds – that big bell, for instance, and the stamping horse. At The Hollies it was the front gate banging and the milk-cart rattling past, the wind in our one tree and the distant sound of builders at work. When the boy had ridden away one of the maids came running into the yard and called: 'Fred, Arthur, come quick. There's been a telegram and they're returning tomorrow.' I heard the man clattering down the steps and ran off home.

Old Nanny had received a telegram too, and the result was that all our hair had to be washed and, to make it shine, ammonia was added to the rinsing water. We sat round the kichen-stove eating dripping toast, wearing towels round our shoulders, while she brushed and combed our hair. We showered her with questions: 'When will they arrive? Will they come by train or car? Will we move into Springfield immediately? Can I take my books, my toys, my bicycle?' And Nanny clicked her teeth and replied: 'I know no more about it than you do. Will you keep your heads still or I shall hit them with the wrong side of the brush.'

We didn't move to Springfield as soon as Mother returned, because we had to wait while bedrooms were being prepared for us and new domestic arrangements made.

When Mother came to The Hollies, it was as if she was a visitor. Her skirts rustled and she wore a gracious air, and instead of unpaid bills her handbag contained a case of visiting cards, a silver-stoppered scent bottle, a little ivory pad with a gold propelling-pencil attached, a gold-net purse and what seemed to us unlimited money. Esmé and I were taken to our friend the tailor and measured for riding habits and to another tailor for tweed coats and skirts, the sort that Grace wore. Almost every day Harrods sent parcels of clothes on approval, kilted skirts and Shetland wool jerseys and little grey suits for Toby. In a short time we were looking exactly like the children in Harrods' catalogues, only we didn't walk about with Mother and Mr Blackwell dressed in our combinations and nothing else or have gentle pillow-fights in camel-hair dressing-gowns. Anyway, however many clothes Mr Blackwell bought, he would never look like a man in a catalogue, and, although being married to Mother had made his moustache grow shorter, he still seemed to me like a Grand Vizier in *The Arabian Nights* or some great bird with a small head and extra long legs – a roc, perhaps.

We left The Hollies the day before Lady Day. Mother came to fetch us in a governess cart that Mr Blackwell had bought her. The tubby white pony that went with it was for us younger ones to ride and the older ones were to share our stepfather's horse for the time being. He said he had given up all idea of being a country gentleman and was grateful to us for taking over the horse.

Since there were not enough large bedrooms to go round, Esmé and I were given adjoining attics on the servants' landing, with sloping ceilings and dormer windows, looking over the churchyard with its crooked gravestones and long, tangled grass. It was a favourite place for birds and they made such a noise in the early morning that we used to think it must be a birds' school, the sparrows the students and the blackbirds and thrushes the teachers, and the big white owl that flew round the churchyard in ever-widening circles at dusk, the headmaster.

We were delighted by our white attics with their highly-polished floors and lamb-skin rugs. There were fitted cupboards for our clothes and treasures, and shelves for our books. We sometimes heard the maids' voices drifting down the landing, yet we far preferred our rooms to the ones on the main landing that had been prepared for John and Polly, although Polly was to sleep in a miniature four-post bed with pink hangings. Clare slept in the room with the puffy eiderdown she had admired so much, but she had to share it with Toby, who was quite capable of waking at six in the morning and demanding to be amused.

We had been told to call Mr Blackwell 'Father', but we couldn't bring ourselves to do that, so we called him Stepfather and later just Step. We were a little shy of him at first and to me it seemed strange and embarrassing that he shared Mother's bedroom and I tried not to think about it. Clare's prophecy that we would see him walking about the landings in his dressing-gown never materialized. He was always downstairs at least an hour before we were, working in his study, where he had his breakfast served. Mother stayed in bed for hers.

There was a silver salver on a console-table in the hall, on which the parlourmaid used to carry visiting cards to Mother. Women I'd never seen before came calling in the afternoons, but the first time they came they weren't offered tea and only stayed a few minutes. Even if a woman called alone, she left a whole bunch of visiting cards, and after they had been lying about for a few days I used to take them and paint miniature pictures on the back – they had a fine surface, almost like ivory. Occasionally Aunt Lawrence came, but she didn't look happy sitting on the gold and white chairs in the drawing-room and, now that it was pointless to advise Mother how to live cheaply, she was rather at a loss. Sometimes she spoke of Ruby, whom she occasionally visited. At last her father had been persuaded to make her an allowance and he had bought Jackson a partnership in a garage. Charles and Aunt Lawrence had made all the arrangements, because Uncle Lawrence still refused to have anything to do with Ruby and her husband and was unlikely to change his mind.

We felt rather as Aunt Lawrence did about the drawing-room chairs. When we first moved into that big house, there was nowhere we could sit or make a mess. Then Mother made us a sitting-room of our own from a large store-room next to the kitchen. It was furnished with some of the furniture from The Hollies and there was a nice old-fashioned fireplace with hobs for keeping things warm on either side and plenty of cupboards. We felt much happier with somewhere of our own and the grown-ups always knocked before entering. The only visitors who did not know the rule were the Irish water-spaniels, and they scratched at the door with their paws. Although they were not allowed in the house, they used to sneak in through the back door, and soon we found we had to share the room with them and step over their huge liver-red bodies when we wanted to sit near the fire. In spite of their curls, they felt the cold.

I think Mother must have envied us our room, because she decided to turn the library into a morning-room. 'The books can stay there, but that long table and those horrible chairs must be put up in the loft – they make the room quite uninhabitable. It would be very different with my sofa and some really comfortable armchairs. I must speak to Edward about it.'

Ever since we had been living at Springfield I hadn't dared to open the library door because of the fearful skin chairs. Sometimes in the night I thought I heard them rumbling and grumbling together and longed to return to the safety of The Hollies. I was happy enough in the daytime as long as I kept well away from the library.

Every morning a tutor called Mr Derbyshire came to teach me for about three hours. I enjoyed the lessons. At last I seemed to be learning; things that I had never understood before became clear. It was as if my mind had been tightly clenched against lesson books. In the afternoons there was the pony to ride, and on Saturday mornings an athletic young woman came and taught us to play tennis. There was some talk about us having French conversation with a nun, but fortunately Mother forgot about this.

I should have been pleased that the chairs were to be banished to the loft, but I wasn't. Now they were doomed, I felt sorry for them, and the rumbling and grumbling at night seemed to become louder. If I sat up in bed and listened, it wasn't there, but, as soon as I lay down, it started again and sometimes I thought there was a kind of chanting. I asked Esmé if she heard noises during the night, but she said she slept like a stone and I didn't like to ask the little ones in case it made them afraid.

One night, as I lay in bed listening to a rumbling, rattling sound, I sat up and could still hear it distinctly. I was only safe from it when I put my head under the clothes. I imagined all the chairs moaning and groaning together because they were to be shut away in the loft and had lost their bodies and souls. As I lay suffocating under the clothes, I remembered Esmé's joking remark about giving the chairs a Christian burial. The more I thought about it, the more the idea pleased me, until I knew it was the only thing to do. I couldn't actually bury the chairs, because they would need such an enormous grave, but I could read the Burial Service over them, and the loft, when they were taken there, would serve as a kind of tomb.

In spite of the sound, I switched on the light, put on my Harrods dressing-gown, not bothering about slippers because it always took so long to find them, slipped my school prayer-

book in my pocket and opened the door. As I did so, the
rumbling-grumbling noises stopped and I seemed to hear a
great sigh. I had to walk down the two flights of stairs in
the darkness, because I did not want to disturb anyone by
showing a light under their bedroom door. I felt extra-
ordinarily brave until I reached the library door, but I dared
not open it for fear I might see something so fearful that I'd
never be the same again. It was completely quiet except for
the hall-clock ticking, no groans or rumbles. I tried looking
through the keyhole, but there was a key in it. Then I opened
the door a little way with my back to it, so that if anything
came out I could run quickly. I slowly turned round and felt
for the light-switch, and under the hard electric light I saw
the chairs dismally gathered round the table, perfectly still
and quiet, but glowering. I had not realized how cold my
feet were until I stepped on to the thick Turkey carpet and
felt the long pile between my toes. I opened the prayer-book
at the Order for the Burial of the Dead and was dismayed to
see how long it was, almost six pages. As I skimmed through
it, I saw there was nothing much I could leave out except
the two Psalms, which seemed a pity, because there were
some beautiful words in them and a lot of wisdom: 'I will
keep my mouth as it were with a bridle, while the ungodly
is in my sight' (something to remember when I was with the
Lawrences), or 'For man walketh in a vain shadow, and dis-
quieteth himself in vain: he heapeth up riches, and cannot
tell who shall gather them.' There was even a homely mention
of a moth fretting a garment.

As I was about to start the service I read in small italics
that people who have not been baptised cannot have a
Christian burial. Now I was faced with two complete services,
besides having to choose six suitable Christian names. I
thought of kings' names at first, but there seemed nothing
but Georges and Edwards and Henrys. Then I noticed a

leather-bound volume of collected poems. It would be nice for the chairs to be called after poets. It took some time to choose names that suited the chairs and appealed to me, but I eventually decided on Percy Shelley. I didn't care for the name Percy, but I loved Shelley and decided that the chair with the lighter skin should be called after him. George Byron was a chair with something slightly wrong with one foot so that it wobbled a bit. Edgar Poe had a mysterious mark running across his skin, as if from a scar. The last three chairs had no distinguishing marks. I called one Alfred Tennyson because it was a good sound name, another William Yeats because he was still alive and I had only recently discovered him, and the third Anon. Circa, who seemed to have died a very long time ago. I read the *Baptism of Such as are of Riper Years* and used water from a flower-vase to cross each chair with as I read: 'I baptise thee in the name of the Father and of the Son and of the Holy Ghost.'

By the time the Baptism Service was over I was feeling terribly tired and my voice had become husky from reading. I sank into Percy Shelley and started on the Burial Service, singing the first part, because it said 'say or sing' and singing made a change. But then there was that long part all about fishes and birds and the twinkling of an eye and the last trump. I only hope I finished the whole service before I fell asleep, leaning forward in Percy Shelley with my head on the table.